The Doppler Effect and Other Stories

The Doppler Effect and Other Stories
by Allen Steele

"Introduction: I Love a Mystery" Copyright © 2017 by Allen M. Steele. Appears in this volume for the first time.

"The Doppler Effect" Copyright © 2017 by Allen M. Steele. Appears in this volume for the first time. (Warren Lapine, editor).

"Frogheads" Copyright © 2015 by Allen M. Steele. Originally published in *Old Venus* (George R.R. Martin and Gardner Dozois, editors), Bantam Books, 2015.

"Einstein's Shadow" Copyright © 2016 by Allen M. Steele. Originally published in *Asimov's Science Fiction* (Sheila Williams, editor), January 2016.

© 2017

This book was first published in electronic format by Positronic Publishing, April 2017.

This is a work of fiction. All the characters and events portrayed in this book are either fictitious or are used fictitiously.

All rights reserved. Printed in the United States of America. No part of this book may be used or reproduced in any manner without written permission except for brief quotations for review purposes only.

Fantastic Books
1380 East 17 Street, Suite 2233
Brooklyn, New York 11230
www.FantasticBooks.biz

ISBN 10: 1-5154-1029-3
ISBN 13: 978-1-5154-1029-4

First Print Edition, August 2017

Contents

Introduction: I Love A Mystery. 7
The Doppler Effect. 11
Frogheads. 85
Einstein's Shadow. 114
About the Author. 162

INTRODUCTION:
I LOVE A MYSTERY

This is a collection of three stories, each a short novel in itself. Strictly speaking, they're science fiction, but that label doesn't describe them accurately. The truth is, when I wrote these stories, I was deliberately playing with a different genre: mystery-suspense fiction.

Science fiction is my first love, in particular the variety commonly known as "hard SF." But I've also read and enjoyed mysteries as well. I don't have much patience for cozy whodunnits or whimsical tales about cats who solve murders, and I often think that if I see another Sherlock Holmes pastiche I'll travel to London and burn a deerstalker cap on Baker Street. But the well-plotted suspense story that keeps me up late turning pages… when I get tired of SF, that's often what I pick up instead.

From the beginning, I've made subtle forays into the mystery genre while staying within the boundaries of science fiction. One of my earliest novellas, "Trembling Earth," was an attempt to do a story about a political assassination plot in which recombinant DNA cloning plays a significant role; the clones in question were dinosaurs, which doesn't sound like an original idea except that my story was published in *Asimov's Science Fiction* a few weeks before Michael Crichton's *Jurassic Park* came out. And some of my novels—*The Jericho Iteration*, *The Tranquility Alternative*, *Oceanspace*, and *V-S Day*—were efforts to write suspense thrillers that also worked as science fiction.

Purists may object, particularly those who'll read nothing but SF and fantasy and disdain all other forms of fiction as "the mainstream." Likewise, there are mystery readers who'd sooner snuggle up with a corpse than a science fiction novel. Yet a trip to any well-stocked secondhand bookstore where you'll find out-of-print books by older writers—more about that in a second—and a close inspection of the SF/F and mystery collections will reveal just how limited that viewpoint really is. Quite a few SF masters—Isaac Asimov, Theodore Sturgeon, Avram Davidson, Fredric Brown, Harlan Ellison, Barry Malzberg, and Kate Wilhelm, to name but a few—also wrote mystery and suspense fiction, sometimes under pseudonym (you know that Sturgeon and Davidson both ghost-wrote Ellery Queen novels, don't you?). Likewise, many authors known mainly for their mysteries—John D. MacDonald, Erle Stanley Gardner, Donald Westlake, Norvell W. Page, Sharyn McCrumb, and yes, even good ol' Sir Arthur Conan Doyle himself—produced SF or fantasy at one point or another in their careers.

In fact, a good case can be made for Edgar Allan Poe being the inventor of *both* SF and mystery fiction. I'll mention as a data point that Poe and I share the same birthday, January 19, and let you draw your own conclusions (such as, I'm a shameless name-dropper).

In recent years, though, there has been much less crossover between the genres. Few writers produce both kinds of fiction. If an author known for SF or fantasy departs from those genres, he or she usually goes no further than, say, supernatural horror fiction or maybe alternative history. Gone are the days when you could pick up the new issue of *Fantasy and Science Fiction* and not be surprised to see a byline you'd normally associate with *Alfred Hitchcock's Mystery Magazine.* A small handful of authors—Walter Mosley, Kristine Kathryn Rush, and Brendan DuBois come to mind—still manage to write either imaginative fiction or crime novels, but not many. And there's a reason for this... just not a good one.

The publishing industry has become much more specialized. In their constant and unending quest to produce nothing but bestsellers all of the time, the major publishing houses have become increasingly oriented toward books that stick within strict genre lines. For this reason, authors who become known for a certain kind of fiction are not encouraged to do anything different. The formula for a career as a bestselling author has become to write a successful novel that falls into a well-defined category, and then write the same sort of novel—or even rewrite that very same book—again and again and again.

So stepping outside genre boundaries is not considered to be a good path for an ambitious young writer. You *might* be able to sell a fantasy novel if you've already done some SF, or vice-versa, but unless you've got such clout that editors are convinced that anything with your name on it will sell boatloads—and really, there are very few authors like that—then your chances of successfully publishing a book that's completely different from your previous work are slim.

And don't even *think* about fusing two genres. The people over in Sales and Marketing will have kittens if you come in with something that they can't describe in five words or less. In today's publishing industry, marketing reps are often involved in editorial decisions about whether or not to buy and publish a particular novel... and sometimes given the last word.

So—as always has been, as always will be—the place for literary experimentation is short fiction, stories that don't belong in Column A, Column B, or Column C. For generations, writers whose ambitions are higher than paying the bills have learned that magazines and anthologies are avenues for work that's not ready for the Amazon Bestseller List. Even so, a writer can run into certain problems if a story they've produced runs up against editorial expectations in regards to genre definitions.

Which brings us to the title story of this collection.

"The Doppler Effect" was originally conceived to be a straightforward SF story, with SETI radioastronomy as its major theme. But when I began to search for a motive for the hoax perpetrated by T-Rex and Princess, I began to realize that, in many ways, this was as a crime story, albeit of the satirical, tongue-in-cheek variety. Not only that, but as I began to work out a way to pull this stunt off—with the help of some very devious friends, I might add—I came to discover that I didn't have to wait for some futuristic technology to be invented years from now, but in fact could use tech that's with us here and now.

The result is a short novel set in the present day that falls squarely between established genres. I like to think that this is what might have been produced by Michael Crichton (in his early pseudonymous "John Lange" period) and Donald Westlake if they'd ever decided to collaborate. There's also some... shall we say, friendly criticism?... of the millennial generation and their dependence on (and abuse of) the social media that may raise a few hackles. This might have made "The Doppler Effect" a difficult story to publish by traditional means; five editors turned it down, even though each of them said that they liked it. You decide.

The next two stories could both be considered alternative history because of their settings. They are that, yes, but I also consider them to be hard-boiled detective stories.

"Einstein's Shadow" is set in an alternative 1930s, aboard the kind of colossal airliner proposed by the futurist designer Norman Bel Geddes as a means of transoceanic air travel. These giant aircraft used to appear fairly frequently in '30s science fiction—read "Piracy Preferred" by John W. Campbell, Jr., or watch the movie *Things to Come*—but became obsolete when aviation technology changed to allow for smaller and more efficient planes like the China Clipper or the DC-3. I decided to revisit the idea in this story, and also write about one of my favorite historic figures in a way that he's not usually depicted. Again, I was working across genre lines. Although this story was published in *Asimov's Science Fiction*, while I was writing it I chose to pretend that it was going to a detective pulp like *Black Mask*. So it's kind of an homage to Dashiell Hammett and Raymond Chandler... and also Walter B. Gibson, née Maxwell Grant, who gets a sly tip of the hat.

"Frogheads" is an even stranger animal. Strictly speaking, it's althistory, too, but that's rather misleading. Really, it's set in something like a parallel dimension; the time period is our own, just with a certain crucial difference. I wrote this for *Old Venus*, an anthology edited George R.R. Martin and Gardner Dozois. The setting is the sort of watery, tropical Venus that often appeared in *Planet Stories* in the '40s, which is what they wanted. So I was thinking about Leigh Brackett and early Ray Bradbury (along with a now-obscure story that appeared in *Planet*, "The Rocketeers Have Shaggy Ears" by Keith Bennett) but also Mickey Spillane and Brett Halliday.

It's a companion to another story I wrote for George and Gardner, "Martian Blood," that appeared in their earlier *Old Mars* book, so you can look for that if you want more of this sort of thing. I'm really hoping those guys edit another anthology like this (although Gardner has sworn that *Old Uranus* will *not* be considered). *Planet Stories* is no longer with us and neither is *Black Mask*, and I'd like to do this sort of thing again.

I'm not sure what you'd call this kind of writing, if you had to give a name to it at all. Hard-boiled space opera, or maybe Noir SF, but please, nothing with the suffix "—punk" at the end. Or better yet, don't bother. Forget labels, relax, and enjoy.

—Whately, Massachusetts
November, 2016

THE DOPPLER EFFECT

The borderlines between fraud, self-deception, gullible acceptance of the fake, and the ideological corruption of science can be very blurred. In theory none of them should happen: in practice, all too often they do, sometimes in combination. Where does one draw the line between, say, self-deception and ideological corruption? The latter may be deliberate and self-serving, but it can equally be a product of the same desire to have reality obey one's wishes....
—John Grant,
Corrupted Science: Fraud, Ideology, and Politics in Science

Never underestimate the power of human stupidity.
—Robert A. Heinlein

The Man in Room 217

On a winter night in rural Massachusetts, the roadside diner looks like a flying saucer that has chosen an exit ramp off I-91 as its landing site. A circular, glass-walled example of Space Age modernism, its frost-rimed windows glow softly in the darkness, resisting the February chill. At the nearby gas station, tractor-trailer rigs idle in the large gravel lot, diesel fumes drifting from their exhaust stacks. Inside the restaurant, truck drivers are huddled over Formica tables, working their way through late dinners before continuing their long hauls north to Canada or south to the Carolinas.

A Ford Escort enters the parking lot. It slowly circles the diner before stopping around back near the kitchen door. A middle-aged black man climbs out. He takes a moment to look about, making sure he's not observed, before walking around front. As he approaches the door, he notices a Subaru hatchback parked midway between the diner and the gas station. The headlights of a passing van sweep across the car, and he catches a glimpse of a figure behind the wheel. Faint wisps from the rear pipe tells him the engine is on, the driver staying warm while he or she waits for someone to show up.

The cowbell above the door jangles as he walks in. Plenty of open tables; with the dinner rush over, the restaurant probably won't get busy again until after midnight, when the overnight drivers come in for a cup of coffee to wash down the bennies that will see them through until morning. He picks a booth as far from the other tables as he can manage, and sits facing the door. He's not hungry, but he picks up the menu and makes a show of looking at it until the waitress comes by.

"Hi there. Coffee?"

"Sure."

A smile and a nod. She's about his age, plump and pleasant looking. Probably been working here for years. "Chilly out there?"

"Yeah, but the road's dry, so…" A shrug finishes the rest. A storm dropped another pile of fresh snow on Western Massachusetts just the other day, adding seven more inches to the thirty-six that had already fallen since the first week of January. He'd come up from New York, and aside from a brief stop at the University of New England campus in Springfield about forty miles down the road, he's been driving all day.

"Nice to know." The waitress steps back from the table. "Specials tonight are American chop suey and Salisbury steak. I'll be back in a sec with the coffee."

She'd just reached the waitress station behind the counter when the cowbell jangles again. The woman who walks in doesn't attract anyone's attention until she lowers the hood of her Bean ski parka. She's young, blonde, and very pretty; the truck drivers stare at her as she walks to the counter.

From where he's sitting, he can hear only a little of what she says to the waitress. Something about picking up a take-out order she'd phoned in a while ago. The waitress checks the order wheel above the kitchen window, has a brief exchange with the cook, then turns to the young woman. "It'll be ready in just a minute, hon. Have a seat, and I'll bring it out to you."

"Thanks." The girl—he pegs her age at eighteen or nineteen—doesn't immediately sit down. Instead, she turns to look around the diner. A couple of truckers try to make eye contact with her, but she ignores them as her gaze settles on the man who'd preceded her into the diner. She hastily glances away, checks the room again, then her eyes return to him.

This time, she doesn't look away, and in that instant, he knows that she's the person he'd been told would be coming to meet him. The girl's face is wary when she walks toward him, her blue eyes cautious for reasons other than those for which young women like her usually are when approaching strange men.

"You're... uh, Mr. Dandridge?" she asks, her voice little more than a whisper.

"Mike Dandridge, yes. Will you join me?" He gestures to the seat across from him; once more she hesitates, glancing about the dining room. "You really ought to sit down," Dandridge says, speaking as softly as she had. "You're going to attract attention, standing around like that."

"Yeah, okay." The girl hastily slides into the booth. "Did you order something?"

"Just coffee. I figured you'd be here soon."

She nods; apparently she doesn't realize that he'd already spotted her. She is little more than a teenager, young enough to be his own daughter if he'd ever had children. She glances over her shoulder, sees that the waitress has just retrieved a grease-stained paper bag from the kitchen window and is ringing it up at the register, and turns to him again.

"All right, Mr. Dandridge," she says quietly, "here's how it is. He's at the motel just down the road from here. Second floor, room 217. After I'm gone, you're going to wait ten minutes, then follow me there. Make sure no one is in back of you. Okay?"

"Yeah, that's fine."

"Awesome."

By then, the waitress has noticed that the girl has moved to Dandridge's table. Drawing a mug of black coffee, she carries it over to the booth along with the take-out order. "Found a friend, I see," she says brightly as she places the coffee before him. She then puts the bag down in front of the girl. "Double diner burger and a large order of fries to go, princess—"

"Don't call me that," the girl mutters, annoyed.

The waitress frowns but says nothing as she lays the check down beside the bag. The girl glances at it, then raises her eyes to Dandridge. "You *are* picking this up, right?"

He's tempted to say no, but decides against it. "Sure."

"Awesome." Princess slips out of the booth. "He's waiting. Don't be late." She plucks the take-out bag from the table and, without so much as a backward glance, hurries to the door. The cowbell announces her departure.

"Sorry about that," Dandridge says to the waitress.

"It's okay. Not your fault." She shakes her head as she peels the receipt off the bag and hands it to him. "Kids…"

"Tell me about it." At least he'd have a chance to drink his coffee. Dandridge pulls out his expense plastic and handed it to the waitress, mentally making a note to tip her well. "Thanks, princess."

The waitress grins. "Awesome," she replies, then strolls back to the register.

The motel is where the girl said it would be, about a quarter-mile down a state road running parallel to I-91. Only a handful of cars and a small moving van are in the lot, parked between snow mounds that look like miniature mountain ranges; there's few tourist attractions in these parts, and the ski areas are many miles away. If this place was the girl's choice for a hideout, then she'd done well. Not many people would look for a fugitive here.

The side entrance is locked, so Dandridge has to go in through the lobby. The guy at the front desk barely notices him. He's transfixed by the flatscreen TV on the lobby wall. As he heads for the stairs, Dandridge catches a snatch of what the desk clerk is watching on CNN:

"Sources at NASA say TKA-01, the source of the mysterious radio transmissions, is closing in on the orbit of Neptune, about two billion and seven hundred million miles from Earth. But while radio observatories around the globe continue to receive signals from the object or objects, all attempts to make contact with TKA-01 have failed so far. Yet scientists at the Jet Propulsion Laboratory in Pasadena, California, remain confident that…"

The stairway door cuts off the rest. Dandridge has heard it before, anyway. TKA-01 has been the top story for the last five weeks, and the major news media outlets think they've got the scoop on what's going on. But if the email he received yesterday is correct, then everything they know is wrong.

Which is why he's here.

Room 217 is halfway down the hall, on the side of the building facing the road. As he stops before the door, he hears the same TV show coming from across the hall. Glancing over his shoulder, he notices that the door to room 216 has been propped open with an empty soda can. He can't see who's in there.

He knocks on 217's door. A few moments pass, then the door opens as far as the security latch will allow. A suspicious blue eye framed by a lock of blond hair peers out at him.

"I'm here," Dandridge says.

The door closes for a moment, the latch is removed, then it swings open again. Princess is there; she'd removed her parka and left it somewhere. She leans forward to cautiously glance up and down the hall, then opens the door wider.

"It's him, Professor," she says, stepping aside.

"Thank you, my dear." The voice is reedy and has a working-class Yankee accent refined by university education: south side of Boston by way of MIT and Cornell, as Dandridge recalls from his research. "You may leave now. I'll call if I need you."

"Awesome." One last, distrustful look, then Princess squeezes past him. Dandridge watches as she steps across the hall and through the door to 216, removing the soda can as she does. The door closes, but Dandridge has the distinct feeling that the girl is still observing him through the peephole.

"Come in, please," the voice says. "I've been waiting for you... Michael C. Dandridge, is it?"

"Only on my byline. Everyone calls me Mike." Dandridge comes the rest of the way into the room, letting the door swung shut behind him. "And you, I take it, are the famous Dr. Theodore Reggs."

The man seated in an armchair on the other side of the room's king-size bed looks like Santa Claus as played by the late, great Zero Mostel. In his early sixties and spectacularly obese, with a hairless scalp and a fluffy, iron-grey beard, he fills the chair in which he sits, his too-small feet propped up on the bed. He wears a red flannel shirt over a tee with Albert

Einstein's face, and the lap of his faded sweat pants is speckled with crumbs. It didn't take very long for him to polish off the double diner burger the girl brought him, for all that remains on the table beside his chair is a sandwich wrapper, a handful of fries, and a Diet Dr. Pepper.

"I am indeed Dr. Reggs. If you'd like, though, you may use the nickname my students and faculty associates... *former* students and faculty associates, that is... call me."

"T-Rex."

"Ah, so you've heard." A smile and a nod. "And before you ask, no, I'm not insulted in the least. Age and diet have given me the dimensions of one of our Jurassic predecessors, but that's not how I earned the sobriquet. Some years ago, some student noticed the way my name was listed in the course catalog—T. Reggs—and how it came out with just the slightest mispronunciation. The nickname stuck, and I must confess that I'm rather fond of it."

"I'll keep that in mind." Dandridge unbuttons his overcoat, but before he takes it off and tosses it on the bed, he pulls out his Sony pocket recorder and notepad. "It'll make a nice detail."

"It might, yes." T-Rex's smile remains, but his eyes narrow. "Have you spoken with anyone about this? The article, I mean."

"Not until I hear what you have to say," Dandridge says as he sits down in the chair at the small desk beside the bed. This is a lie. He'd already spoken with several people at the university. There was no reason, though, why Dr. Reggs should know this. "If I think there's something here," he goes on, "then I'll get in touch with one of the magazines I write for—*Atlantic*, *Rolling Stone*, maybe *The New Yorker*—and see if they're interested."

"Of course." T-Rex slowly nods. "You're a freelancer, so I'm sure that it's prudent to hear what a source has to say before pitching an article to an editor. In fact, I'm relieved that you haven't talked to anyone else. There's a reason why I'm hiding out here, y'know."

"I've been wondering about that."

"The university is no longer safe for me. Nor is my house." He sighs and looks away. "You probably think you know the reason why... the public reaction following the announcement of TKA-01. Truth is, though, UNE wasn't safe for me even before this whole thing got started."

As Dr. Reggs speaks, Dandridge silently points to his recorder and notepad. T-Rex nods again, and Dandridge picks them up, switches on the recorder, and opens the notepad. "I'm sure you've had little privacy since making the announcement," he says as he pulls a pen from his shirt pocket, "but you'd think the fame—"

"There's fame, and then there's infamy. Very soon, I'm afraid, one will become the other. That's why I've gone into hiding, with only one of my former students knowing where I am."

"The girl?" Dandridge cocks his head in the direction of Princess's room.

"Yes. I'd just as soon keep her out of this, though, if I can. There's no reason why her reputation should be ruined along with mine."

Dandridge raises an eyebrow. "Your reputation? That's pretty solid, I should think. After all, aren't you the discoverer of TKA-01? The scientist who's confirmed the existence of intelligent life in the universe?"

Theodore Reggs, Professor of Physics at the University of New England and one of the foremost authorities on the search for extraterrestrial intelligence, doesn't respond at once. The drapes of the window behind them are closed; leaning back in his chair, he reaches over to pull one of them a few inches aside and take a peek at the parking lot. Dandridge's car is there, but he'd taken the precaution of parking as far from the building as he could, away from the light posts. T-Rex studies the lot for a few moments, then lets the drape fall back in place. Looking at Dandridge again, he slowly lets out his breath.

"TKA-01 is a fake," he says. "It's nothing but a goddamn hoax."

Oh, Be A Fine Girl, Kiss Me

Six months earlier…

A short, loud buzz outside his office told him that the class period was over and the next would begin in ten minutes. T-Rex—he'd long since stopped thinking of himself by any other name, even Ted—sighed in mild annoyance. He'd returned to teaching only a couple of weeks ago, and he hadn't completely readjusted to the daily routine of academic life. Two years away from the classroom had played havoc with his mental schedule; he needed to get used to the idea that his time was no longer solely his own.

Regretting the end of his sabbatical, and fondly contemplating the prospect of retirement in a few more years, he saved the lecture notes he'd been fine-tuning, closed his MacBook, then heaved himself up from the antique doctor's chair he'd brought to this office many years ago. Miraculously, it had remained untouched while he was gone, with one notable exception. It helped that the university had locked his office and left it undisturbed. Otherwise, the oak swivel chair—the only piece of office furniture he'd found that was both comfortable and solid enough to sustain his mass—might have disappeared into someone else's office.

He had little doubt as to who would have taken it.

One more glance about an office that seniority assured would never have to be shared with another faculty member, then T-Rex picked up his computer and lumbered out into the hall. Undergraduates rushing to their next class stepped around him as he made his ponderous way down the corridor. Following his doctor's advice not to do anything that might put a strain on his heart, T-Rex never hurried anywhere. He'd been given a dinosaur's name, but in actual fact he was more like a woolly mammoth.

Just before he reached the elevator that would take him down to the classrooms and lecture halls, he passed a half-dozen students waiting outside another office. As he sauntered by, T-Rex glanced through the open door. A handsome young Latino associate professor sat at his desk, leaning forward slightly as he listened intently to a nervous female student. The younger man looked up as his senior colleague walked past.

"Good morning, Dr. Reggs."

"Dr. Tuleja." A short, even reply.

T-Rex didn't stop to talk. Even if doing so wouldn't have made him late for class, the last person whom he wanted to chat with was Luis Tuleja. He was quite attractive, yes—the girl sitting across the desk from him was practically drooling—but T-Rex had reason to keep his distance besides the fact that Luis was unquestionably straight.

It wasn't for nothing that he'd learned to guard his chair. And his job.

T-Rex turned his mind toward more immediate matters... namely, this morning's Astronomy 101 lecture. As payback for his prolonged sabbatical from teaching, he'd agreed to take over the entry-level astronomy course for the fall semester from its usual instructor, Jodi McCabe. Jodi was the department chair, but she still enjoyed teaching the rudiments to undergraduates. However, this semester she was putting the finishing touches on a major paper she was co-authoring for *Physics Review* and needed the extra time. It had been years since the last time T-

Rex had done this sort of grunt work, but the students seemed interested enough, although a few seemed to be here mainly because they loved *Star Wars*. Only last week, one of them had raised a hand and asked, with a completely straight face, which galaxy was the location for the Dagobah system.

"Too many movies you have seen, hmm?" T-Rex replied.

His Yoda impression wasn't half-bad, and in years past it would've earned him a laugh, but this time it was received with a sullen glare from the student who'd asked the question, and cold silence from his classmates. T-Rex had heard that college students had lately become thin-skinned and rather humorless, but until then he hadn't believed it. Teaching is hard work, but it's also supposed to be fun, and when imitating Yoda gets the stiff upper lip treatment... well, maybe it was time to hang it up. This wasn't the first time the thought had crossed his mind lately.

The students had already taken their seats when he arrived. Holding onto the handrail running along one side of the lecture hall, T-Rex made his way down to the lectern. He took a minute to plug in his computer and pull up his notes and slides, and as the screen beside him lit to display the first page of today's lecture—*Major Stellar Types and Their Classifications*, backlit by a lovely photo of M-104, the Sombrero Galaxy—the buzz of conversation gradually subsided and the twenty-five students enrolled in this year's Astronomy 101 seminar turned their attention to their teacher.

T-Rex began with the observation that, when one looks up at the night sky, it can sometimes appear that all the stars seem much the same, with the only difference being that some are a little brighter than others or have slightly different hues. In reality, though, stars have quite a few different sizes and colors; those differences are the result of age, mass, luminosity, and surface temperature.

Sliding his finger across the MacBook touchpad, T-Rex opened the next screen on his PowerPoint menu. Upon the screen appeared the Hertzsprung-Russell diagram, a slightly curved line running downward from right to left within a right-angle formed by two axes. Plucking a laser pointer from his shirt pocket, T-Rex began explaining the diagram. The curve in the center was the main sequence; it was comprised of the most common types of stars, with the brightest stars at the upper left and the dimmest at the lower right. The vertical y-axis bar on the left showed, in ascending order, the absolute magnitudes of various stellar types on a scale from 15 to -10. Running across the horizontal x-axis bar at the bottom of the graph were the major spectral types. From left to right, they were labeled O, B, A, F, G, K, and M.

"All visible stars except for galaxies, stellar clusters, planets, and minor planets are classified by spectral type," T-Rex said. "There are seven different kinds of stars, and they're listed in this order." He pointed the laser at the x-axis bar. "There's an easy way to remember them, by the way: 'Oh, Be A Fine Girl, Kiss Me.'"

It was a traditional mnemonic that he'd learned himself many years ago as a freshman. Students usually received this tidbit with a few appreciative chuckles. On occasion, T-Rex had seen male students turn to young ladies sitting beside them and reiterate the line, just to see if they'd get the desired response.

This time, though, the reaction was different.

Wide-eyed surprise. Angry glares. No smiles, no laughter, not even so much as a giggle. The silence was broken only by a few whispered comments he couldn't make out. Then a hand went up from the second row, raised by a pretty young blonde. He couldn't recall her name; this early in the semester, he hadn't yet had memorized those of his new students.

T-Rex pointed to her. "Yes?"

"Dr. Reggs, I'm sorry, but I'm offended."

"By what?"

"What you just said... it's offensive."

T-Rex blinked. He fully understood what she'd said; what she meant, though, was baffling. "You're offended by 'Oh, Be A Fine Girl, Kiss Me'?" he asked, and she nodded. "In what way?"

"It's degrading." As she spoke, several other girls in the lecture hall nodded vigorously. Much to T-Rex's surprise, so did a few boys. "Women need to be treated with respect, professor. We're not sex objects."

"I didn't say you were." T-Rex tried hard not to smile, but didn't quite succeed. "It's simply a way of remembering the major spectral types. Astronomers have been using it for years." He allowed himself a chuckle. "Surely, an attractive young lady such as yourself has been kissed at least once, have you not?"

As soon as he said this, he knew that he'd made a mistake. The girl's mouth fell open and her face turned bright red; several other females reacted as if they'd just been pinched. "That's none of your business!" she exclaimed. "I want an apology!"

"Very well." Quietly sighing under his breath, T-Rex held up a hand in a placating manner. "If you feel that way, then I'm sorry."

Although she still appeared to be irate, the girl nodded in reluctant acceptance. There was still tension in the room, though, with several students continuing to glare at him. T-Rex decided to try a little humor. "If it makes you feel any better," he added, "you could always change it to, 'Oh, Be A Fine Guy, Kiss Me.'"

As her mouth dropped open, T-Rex realized too late that his attempt to resolve the matter had backfired. As low, unamused mutters spread throughout the hall, students furiously tapped at their keyboards. A couple pulled out their smartphones and held them up, their lenses aimed in his direction. Three rows back from the girl who'd spoken, a young man with purple-streaked hair and a bodybuilder's physique stood up without first raising his hand.

"Professor Reggs, as a member of the university's LGBT community—"

"You are?" T-Rex smiled at the handsome young lad. "Welcome. Glad to have you aboard."

"—I'm offended, too. Comments like that are problematic. Frankly, they're homophobic, and therefore unacceptable."

T-Rex stared at him. Either the kid hadn't heard what he'd just said or it had gone over his head. "All right, then," he said, speaking slowly, "how about 'Oh, Be A Fine Gay, Kiss Me'? Better now?" He thought for a second. "Or if you're Jewish," he added, "you could always say to your gentile friend, 'Oh, Be A Fine Goy, Kiss Me.'"

Loud hisses, along with several boos. Another student shot to his feet. "Dr. Reggs, as a Jew, I *insist* on an apology!"

"Really?" T-Rex knew at once that it would be futile to point out that he, too, belonged to the tribe. "Well, you're not going to get it. A joke is a joke, and if you can't take one, then it's not my fault. Now sit down and be quiet... I have a class to teach."

The student who'd just raised his voice snatched up his iPad and daypack and stormed out of the room. Just before he reached the door, he stopped to look back at him. If he was still expecting an apology, though, T-Rex wasn't about to offer one. If anything, the professor was angry enough to consider throwing him out of the class for good and giving him an Incomplete for the semester grade. But he said nothing, and as he looked at his notes again to recall what he'd been talking about, he heard the door bang open and slam shut.

That should have ended the matter, but it didn't. A few minutes later, another hand went up. This time it was a male student a few rows back from the center. "Dr. Reggs, I'm disturbed by the term for the stars you just mentioned."

"What?" T-Rex turned away from the H-R diagram still on the screen. "M-class stars?"

"Yeah. You call them red dwarfs."

"That's right. They're M-class red dwarfs." T-Rex ran his pointer's tiny amber spot from the handful of dots at the diagram's bottom right side to another handful at the bottom left side. "Just as these are white dwarfs... much the same magnitude, but off the main sequence. I don't understand. How is this—?"

"Don't you believe that calling them 'red dwarfs' and 'white dwarfs' is a form of microaggression?" The student who spoke had a shaved head and a long hipster beard, his neck and arms covered with tattoos. T-Rex remembered when the only time you ever saw a chap like that was when he was standing between the wild man of Tasmania and the Siamese twins. "That is, appropriating certain terms to distinguish people of color... in this instance, Native Americans... from the white majority in order to further their racial oppression?"

"No, I don't." What he couldn't believe was that he was even having this discussion. T-Rex sought to keep a level tone. "These particular terms are used by astronomers for these particular stars because, when you view them through a telescope, they're white and red. Their colors are the result of age, mass, and surface temperature, and have nothing to do with racism, white supremacy, the Battle of Little Bighorn, or—"

Once again, the lecture hall erupted in boos and hisses. "Oh, come on!" T-Rex snapped, addressing no one in particular. "Are you going to tell me that you object to them being called dwarfs, too?"

"They're not dwarfs!" someone yelled. "They're vertically challenged!"

Now it was T-Rex's turn to have his jaw fall open. "So now we're supposed to call M-class stars 'vertically challenged stellar objects of color'? The IAU would love that."

"Then the IAU is a hate group!" someone else shouted.

Apparently he wasn't aware that the initials stood for International Astronomical Union. On the other hand, it was possible that he did and actually believed what he said. Either way, T-Rex realized that this morning's lecture was a lost cause and there was no point in going on.

"This discussion is absurd." T-Rex disconnected his MacBook, shut it, and tucked it under his arm. "Class dismissed." Leaving the lectern, he marched up the aisle, ignoring the hostile stares from either side of the room.

He thought that would be the end of it. He was wrong.

Monster on Campus

"Did it get worse?" Dandridge asks.

"Oh, yes... and rather quickly, too." T-Rex picks up his Diet Dr. Pepper and takes a sip. "When I came to work the next morning, I found that someone had spray-painted a swastika on my office door." A bleak and humorless smile. "Y'know, as a Jewish liberal gay college professor, the last thing I ever thought would happen was to be accused of being a Nazi. But that wasn't all. By then, I was also—"

Peering up at the ceiling, he begins to tick off his fingers. "Let's see... sexist, racist, homophobic, anti-Semitic, and achondroplasiaphobiac—"

"Achondro... what?"

"Achondroplasiaphobia... fear of dwarves. Pardon me, 'little people.' Yeah, I had to look it up, too. I was also a right-wing Republican even though anyone who's ever seen my car can't miss the old Bernie Sanders sticker on the back." He snaps his fingers as if remembering something. "Oh, and one person speculated that I might even belong to the Ku Klux Klan. No proof of any of this, of course, but on the other hand, none was asked for."

He pats his belly. "Incidentally, the people who accused me of all these things had no problem finding ways to describe my girth. 'Fat ass' was the mildest. I have to admit, though, I'm rather fond of 'fascist pig from outer space.' At least it showed some creativity."

"And where did you see all these comments?"

"Where else? On the Internet. Blogs, discussion groups, the usual. I didn't realize it at the time, but some students were tweeting about the lecture even as it was happening. One of the kids also recorded everything with his smartphone. The first blog posts were already up before I left the room, and an edited version of my lecture appeared by lunchtime. It had gone viral by the end of the day, with one site scoring over fifty thousand hits."

"Wow."

"Yeah… wow. When I found out about this, I went online and Googled myself. The first posts were on UNE's campus server, of course, but quite a few were on places that had no association with the university at all. Judging from the authoritative nature of the opinions, it appears that two or three hundred people attended my lecture that morning. Everyone had heard me with their own ears when I ridiculed women, gays, Jews, and people of color."

"And dwarves."

"And dwarves… how can I forget?" There's a cold French fry still on the table. T-Rex absently dabs it in a puddle of ketchup on the sandwich wrapper and sticks it in his mouth. "I expected the whole thing to blow over. The lecture happened on Thursday morning. The weekend was coming up, so I figured things would simmer down. I was prepared to go into next Tuesday's lecture and apologize for anything that might have offended anyone. But it didn't blow over. The swastika on my door was just the first indication that the reaction was about to go way beyond blogs and tweets."

"There were protests, weren't there?"

"Over the weekend, a couple of university activist groups organized an anti-hate rally. Monday at noon, the students staged a march in the campus quadrangle, ending in a sit-in at the administration building. The protesters weren't there very long. The little darlings didn't want to skip lunch, and I'm told that Monday is mac and jalapeno day at the student union. But it lasted long enough for their spokesperson to visit the president's office and present a petition calling for my immediate dismissal."

T-Rex pauses to look out the window. "But it wasn't the rally that did the most damage, or even the student petition," he adds after a moment, still peering past the drapes. "It was the second petition that hurt the most. That's the one I didn't see coming."

"From the students?"

"No, from someone a lot closer." When T-Rex looks away from the window again, his face is grim. "My colleagues... one in particular."

During the 1970s, at the height of the campus demonstrations against the Vietnam War, the University of New England demolished the original administration building that had been there since the antebellum period following the Civil War and replaced it with a more modernistic structure. In response to the times, architects designed the flat-roofed concrete building to withstand siege by student protesters. There were no windows on the ground floor, only shatterproof Plexiglass doors; the windows on the second and third floors were narrow slots resembling those of a medieval European castle. There was even an underground tunnel connecting the building with the adjacent parking garage, enabling administrators and staff members to enter their workplace without going outside.

T-Rex always thought of this particular architectural style as Post-Apocalypse Americana: ugly, functional, and cynical. But just then, standing in the window of the top floor conference room, he found himself grateful for where the university president's offices were located. He'd parked his Jeep in the garage and come in through the tunnel so that the students gathered in the plaza outside wouldn't observe his arrival, just as they wouldn't see him peering down at them from behind the Venetian blinds of a third-floor conference room window.

At the moment, there were only a couple out there. It was an overcast, drizzly morning, one full week after the lecture that had landed him in trouble. Perhaps the weather was keeping the numbers down, or maybe it was just the necessity of having to attend classes every once in a while. But the kids weren't going away entirely, and neither were their signs.

"I like that one." T-Rex pointed to the cardboard sign—*Make T-Rex Extinct!*—held by a young black man in dreadlocks and a dungaree jacket. "At least the sign shows some originality."

"You're very forgiving, Ted." Standing beside him, Jodi McCabe gazed down at the rotund girl with a buzz cut holding the sign reading *Reggs = RACIST!* "That's utterly false, and I bet she knows it, too."

A trim, petite woman in her mid-sixties with iron-grey hair, wire-frame glasses, and a Kentucky accent toned down by years of living in the Northeast, Jodi McCabe looked every inch the person she was, a lifelong academic who was the head of UNE's physics department. She was also one of his oldest friends; he'd known her for decades, ever since they'd both joined the faculty at about the same time this building opened its doors for the first time.

A good woman to have on his side. He could only hope that it was enough.

"She might," T-Rex said, "or she might not." As they watched, the girl called over her companion, then pulled out a smartphone and used it to take a selfie of the two of them. "Chances are she really believes what she's read, and that I'm a racist, homophobic, anti-Semitic, dwarf-kicking—"

The door opened, and he stopped himself as two men walked in. The first he recognized only slightly. T-Rex had met David Rycroft, the university president, just once before—and then only briefly—at the faculty reception shortly after he'd come to UNE a few years ago. In his early fifties, athletically slender from regular exercise on the university's handball courts, Rycroft was a familiar type, an academic bureaucrat who seldom set foot in a class room but had instead risen to his position by an ability to raise money and charm important alumni.

The second person, unfortunately, was all too familiar: Luis Tuleja. For today's meeting, Luis had decided to put on his best suit and tie. Seeing him, T-Rex suddenly regretted his usual outfit of Old Navy jeans, flannel shirt, and Indian trading post moccasins. But it was the expression on Tuleja's face—like that of a prosecuting attorney showing up for court—that made him realize that this meeting was probably not going to have a good outcome regardless of what he was wearing.

"Good morning, Professor Reggs, Professor McCabe." Rycroft favored them with a formal smile as he gestured to the long conference table running down the center of the room. "If you'll please be seated..." He glanced at the executive assistant who'd followed him from his office. "Hold my calls, please. And would you have Marley bring us some coffee? Thanks."

Rycroft was doing his best to make everyone feel at ease and equal to one another, but T-Rex knew an inquisition when he saw one coming.

There was a predatory look in Tuleja's eyes like that of a cat who'd cornered a mouse it had already injured. Rycroft wasn't aware of what was going on here—what was *really* going on—and it was possible that Jodi either didn't or refused to acknowledge it. But T-Rex knew, and so did Luis.

"Let's get started," Rycroft said as everyone took their places at the table, himself at the head. "Needless to say, the university is embarrassed by the attention this affair has brought us. I'm worried that it might cast the school in a bad light, and if it continues unabated it may cost us our reputation."

"I'm sorry for all this, Dr. Rycroft—" T-Rex began.

"Actually, it's Mr. Rycroft. Thanks for the compliment, but I'm the only person in the room who doesn't have a doctorate." He smiled. "In any case, let's keep this informal, Ted… call me David, please."

"Of course." T-Rex kicked himself for the *faux pas*. "As I saying… I'm sorry for any embarrassment this incident may have caused, but if you've seen the smartphone footage from my lecture that was posted on YouTube, surely you must be aware that certain things… the questions I was asked, some key words in my response… were deleted, edited out to make what I said seem worse than they actually were."

"Yes, I have." Rycroft nodded toward Jodi. "Dr. McCabe… Jodi… pointed this out to me in the first meeting I had with her about this."

"So you know the truth. I didn't make any bigoted statements during my lecture. I'd repeated a commonly-used mnemonic, 'Oh, Be A Fine Girl, Kiss Me,' that one student mistook as a sexist remark, and the situation escalated from there." He shrugged. "If I'm guilty of anything, it's making a bad joke. That's all."

Tuleja frowned but remained quiet. "I agree, those are the facts," Rycroft said, "but as much as I hate to say it, truth and facts are no longer the issue. The problem is that, like all big public universities, UNE depends on endowments, and those endowments come only if its departments are in good standing in the academic and scientific communities. You've seen the student paper, haven't you?"

"Yes, I have." A front-page editorial, with the headline "Monster on Campus" running above an unflattering photo of himself, had called for his immediate dismissal on the grounds of the sexist and racial slurs he'd allegedly made. "I hope you're not taking their demands seriously."

"Surely you can't be," Jodi said. "The kids have blown this all out of proportion. You know that."

"I'm sorry, Jodi," Rycroft said, "but I have to take it seriously. The petition, the rally, the ongoing demonstration outside this building... this incident could hurt the school very badly." His gaze drifted in Tuleja's direction. "And it's not just the student body. As I'm sure you're both already aware, yesterday afternoon a second petition was sent to my office. This one comes from the faculty. Twenty faculty members have called for your resignation, Ted—"

"I know." T-Rex's voice hardened. "I haven't seen it myself, but I think I can guess whose name was at the top of the list."

Although he'd been gone from campus for the last couple of years, T-Rex had kept an ear to the faculty grapevine. So he knew that a member of the physics department, in his absence, had been lured from a similar position at the University of Arizona. And from the beginning, long before he actually met Dr. Luis Tuleja, he'd learned not to trust him.

Shortly after Tuleja arrived on campus, he'd attempted to steal T-Rex's prized doctor's chair. Apparently Luis had persuaded a custodian to open T-Rex's office and let him take a chair from it, since there hadn't been one in his own office when he'd moved in. The theft was discovered by Jodi when she'd dropped by for a visit. She'd firmly told Dr. Tuleja to return Dr. Reggs's chair, and he'd had done so without argument—*I thought it was abandoned* was his excuse—but more than just this minor incident gave T-Rex cause to distrust the newest member of the physics faculty.

It was no secret that Jodi was planning to retire in another year or so. If rumors were true, Luis coveted the job. Although he was new to the faculty, he'd quickly become a rising star at UNE, popular among students and highly respected by his colleagues. And since Dr. Reggs's seniority all but assured that he'd be the first in the line of succession, Tuleja perceived him as an obstacle.

The truth of the matter, though, was that T-Rex didn't want the job. He was looking forward to retirement himself, and thus intended to continue teaching at UNE only long enough to ensure that he'd receive a nice pension. But Luis was young and ambitious, and keenly desired the position for which T-Rex was ambivalent. He'd learned which buttons to push among his fellow faculty members, and had done a good job of pushing them.

Not only that, but while T-Rex had become seldom seen at UNE during the period it had taken for him to get Project MARVIN up and running, Luis had gained prominence through the university's participation in NASA's MarsCube program. Because MarsCube 4 was designed and built by Luis's students, they'd gone on a university-paid trip to Cape Canaveral last March to watch it and five other MarsCubes get launched aboard a SpaceX Falcon 9, after which they'd retreated to Cocoa Beach where the budding young scientists had celebrated with beer pong. In this way, Dr. Tuleja had become quite popular among the students. No wonder there was a line outside his office.

All the same, Luis's ambitions were beneath T-Rex's attention. He'd been on the UNE faculty for thirty-three years, a tenured professor for the last twenty-one. Not only was he respected among his colleagues, but he was also regarded as a leading expert in the SETI field, a protégé of the late Philip Morrison. Once he retired to Provincetown on Cape Cod, he intended to spend his days cheerfully ignoring his doctor's advice about alcohol intake as he searched for a younger man willing to keep a fat old queen company. So if Luis yearned to take over the physics department… well, let him. Now that MARVIN had reached operating status, T-Rex was looking forward to becoming a professor emeritus.

Or so he'd believed.

Now, gazing across the conference room table at the fellow teacher who'd become his adversary, T-Rex realized that Luis Tuleja had taken an incident that might have blown over and, through artful manipulation of faculty politics and social media, had engineered a coup. He wouldn't have to wait until T-Rex retired to become Jodi's successor. All he had to do was take advantage of a bad situation.

"It's nothing personal, Dr. Reggs… Ted, I mean." Luis's expression was just sympathetic enough to be convincing. "Even if your remarks weren't made in ernest—" a sidelong glance a Jodi "—and I'm willing to give you the benefit of the doubt—"

"Thanks," T-Rex said drily.

"—it still puts everyone in a bad position. As David said, we're all dependent on grant money to conduct our research. MarsCube 4, for instance, is entirely supported by outside funds. If the non-profit foundations and private corporations furnishing that money come to believe that their reputations may be smeared by this, particularly if there's a lawsuit involved—"

"A lawsuit?" Jodi was incredulous. "Oh, really now, Luis…"

"I'm afraid he's right," Rycroft said. "This morning, I heard from the university's attorney, telling me that a civil rights organization representing the student groups who've been staging the protests is threatening to lodge a Title IX complaint against the university."

"Title IX? You mean the Equal Opportunity in Education Act?" Jodi raised an eyebrow when the president nodded an affirmative. "But isn't this supposed to guarantee equal access to collegiate sports facilities by female athletes? Like, making sure that the girl's field hockey team can use the gym showers, too?"

"It is, but lately it's been used to address other gender issues on college campuses. When Ted made his remarks about kissing girls and kissing boys and kissing gay men—"

"*I'm* a gay man, forchrissakes!" T-Rex snapped. "And how many times do I have to explain this? 'Oh, Be A Fine Girl, Kiss Me' is—"

"A way of remembering different kinds of stars. Yes, I know that. But some female students in your class felt threatened—"

"*Threatened?*"

"—by the loss of their safe space, and that's brought us to where we are today. Bad press, loss of funding, a possible civil rights lawsuit—"

"And let's not forget the loss of academic freedom. Or does that count anymore?"

"Nobody's forgetting anything." Rycroft slowly let out his breath. "Ted, I believe you when you say it was all a joke that the kids took too seriously. Really, I do. But Luis is right. The university is in an untenable position here, and…"

His voice trailed off and he looked away. There was a soft knock on the door, then it opened and a well-groomed student intern wearing a coat and tie came in bearing a coffee tray. The conversation paused while he placed it on the conference table, but although he left without a word, T-Rex couldn't help but notice the hostile glance the kid threw in his direction. No doubt, as soon as he closed the door, he'd tweet all his friends about how he'd just seen Satan sitting in President Rycroft's office. So much for a private meeting.

"I think I know where this is leading," T-Rex said once the intern was gone. "I'm fired, right?"

"No." Still not looking at him, Rycroft shook his head. "Not necessarily. But your resignation would be appreciated, and it would save everyone a lot of trouble."

T-Rex sighed, then looked down at the table and slowly nodded. Feeling Jodi take his hand, he looked at her. There were tears in the corners of her eyes and her lips were trembling, and once again he realized how much he loved her. Even David Rycroft seemed sympathetic; his remorseful expression was that of a man who'd been forced to make a painful decision.

And meanwhile, across the table, it wasn't hard to tell that Luis Tuleja was trying hard to keep from smiling.

The Apology Trap

The swastika was still on the door when he returned to his office. Apparently the university's buildings and grounds department hadn't yet gotten around to sanding it off. T-Rex did his best to ignore it as he fished his keyring from his pocket. He didn't bother to shut the door behind him, but instead stood there for a moment, letting his gaze travel around the room.

It wasn't a large office but it was comfortable, with a good view of the spired dome of the campus library visible beyond a handsome stand of oaks that had probably been there since the original state college was founded in the 1860s. He'd brought in bookcases, framed posters of astronomical images, potted ferns, a nice Indian rug he'd bought cheap at a flea market, and over time it had transformed into a pleasant den, less academic than the usual faculty office.

He'd occupied this place for... how long? T-Rex had to think about it for a moment. He'd moved in right after the Goddard Physics Building was built, and that was almost twenty-five years ago. By then he'd already been teaching at UNE for nearly a decade. That long.

He'd need boxes to pack everything. A lot of boxes. And someone to help him with the furniture, too. The desk and bookcases belonged to the university, but the armchair was his. So was the big quartz astrolabe mounted in a brass globe-stand over in the corner. Engraved with the major constellations, it been presented to him by Jodi and the rest of the physics department some years ago when he'd reached his twenty-fifth year teaching at the university. A reminder of happier times. It was heavy and fragile, and it would be a bitch to move, but he was damned if he was going to leave it behind and let Luis inherit it.

First, though, he'd need to collect some liquor cartons for all his books, files, and belongings, and rent a U-Haul truck, and enlist some undergraduates to help him schlep everything home...

The last might be a problem, if the swastika was an indication of how the student body felt about him these days.

T-Rex sat down heavily in his chair. God, how had it come to this?

He sat there for a long time, feeling numb, still trying to absorb the meeting he'd just come from. David Rycroft had been almost apologetic as he and Jodi were walking out the door. *Off the record, Ted, I know this isn't your fault. But we can't keep you here. The political climate these days, the culture wars... really, I wish there was more I could do.*

T-Rex closed his eyes, shook his head. "Sure there is, David," he murmured under his breath, repeating what he'd said no more than a half-hour ago. "You could do the right thing and stand up for your teachers." But that would mean having some balls, wouldn't it?

For lack of anything better to do, he switched on his computer and logged into UNet, the campus server. Until a week ago, he'd received only a dozen or so emails a day, usually questions from students about assignments or routine departmental notices, along with the occasional invitation to a faculty barbecue or cocktail party. Since The Lecture—as he'd come to think of it, to distinguish it from the countless other classroom lectures he'd given in his career without incident—his box had been stuffed with hundreds of notes from students, the vast majority of them anonymous because UNet allowed students to use it without providing their own names, each of them telling what a vile, hate-filled person he was and how he deserved to be fired or die, not necessarily in that order.

T-Rex ran the cursor down the list, skipping the ones with headers like *YourLechture* and *Evil Asshole* and *Why Do U Hate Queers?*, until he landed on something that looked like it might actually offer a breath of good news. Marked *SETI Conference Participation*, it had been sent by the academic organization sponsoring an upcoming science conference to which he'd been invited to deliver a talk about MARVIN. Besides the fact that he'd get to see a lot of old friends in the astronomical community, the conference was scheduled for early January on Pawley's Island in South Carolina, a nice place to get away from the snows of New England in the first month of winter. And God knew that he needed some moral support from...

That thought died as he opened the email. Not quite believing what he saw, he had to read it two more times before he truly believed what he'd just received. It came from the conference chairperson, and it began:

Dear Dr. Reggs:

The organizing committee of the upcoming SETI Summit has recently learned of the controversy surrounding remarks alleged to have been made by you during a classroom lecture at the University of New England. Although we respect the views of all our members, the organization's charter and the conference itself has a strict "no tolerance" stance against any written or verbal statements that reflect racial or sexual discrimination by prospective speakers.

Because of this, we greatly regret to inform you that your invitation to address the upcoming conference is being rescinded, and that your program item will be removed from our schedule of...

"Cowards." Reading the letter for the third time, the words finally slipped from his lips. "Those goddamn fucking cowards—"

"Excuse me... Dr. Reggs?"

Startled by the voice from the doorway, he jerked slightly in his chair as he looked up from the computer screen. A young woman was standing there: young, blonde, very pretty, and—judging from her red-faced, wide-eyed expression—embarrassed by what she'd just heard him say.

T-Rex recognized her as one of his undergraduate students. It took him another moment, though, to specifically recognize which one she was. For although he wouldn't have remembered her name if someone had pointed a gun to his head, he realized that this was the very same student who, almost exactly one week ago, had raised her hand to object to the mnemonic for stellar classifications.

They stared at each other for a few seconds, neither of them knowing quite what to say. Then T-Rex found the words that broke the spell.

"Hello. Come to celebrate?" He was tempted to ask her to be a fine girl and drop dead, but decided that he'd better not. Given the subject lines of all the emails he'd just received, he might be chased off campus by students carrying torches and pitchforks until they cornered him in an abandoned windmill on the outskirts of town.

"Celebrate?" She gave him a curious look. "Why would I want to do that?"

"I suppose the news hasn't reached you yet." How odd to realize that he wasn't angry with her, even though she'd started the whole mess. She was just a silly girl who'd said a silly thing; it's hard to hate someone for that. "I've been terminated. More precisely, I've been strongly encouraged to tender my resignation... which I have." He shrugged. "They could've fired me, of course, but I was told that, if I left quietly without a fuss, I could at least retain my pension and status as professor emeritus, along with a couple of other privileges."

This was a small consolation, at least. Because President Rycroft had agreed to let him retain emeritus status, he was able to continue using university resources for MARVIN. This was a relief; he might no longer have an office at the university, but he'd still have access to his creation.

"But you're not teaching here anymore?" the girl asked.

"No, I'm not." Forcing a smile, he gazed at his former student, whose name he still didn't know. "You win. The monster has been vanquished. Your world is safe again."

"I... I... I..." Her face went pale as she groped for words. "I didn't want you to lose your job!" she blurted out, and T-Rex was surprised to see tears forming in her eyes. "I just wanted you to apologize and—"

She stopped abruptly, as if about admit something she shouldn't. "You got your apology," T-Rex prodded, more confused than angry. "I gave it to you at once. What else did you want from me?"

"An A."

He stared at her. "What?"

She looked down at the floor. "That's the way it works... don't you know? If a teacher says something offensive, he apologizes for it. And then to make up for it, he gives you an A. That's what I thought you'd... I mean, that's the way it always—"

"Oh, no, it does not. Not in my classroom." Something went cold in him. "Wait... was that what everyone expecting from me?"

"Sure." The girl slowly nodded, still unable to look at him. "UNE students do it all the time. You listen hard to what the prof is saying, pick out something that could be racist or sexist or whatever, and then make like you're really, really offended. That forces him to apologize, and then just to make sure that you don't keep going after him about it—"

"He assuages your poor, hurt feelings by giving you an A." The old armchair creaked loudly as T-Rex sagged back it in. Unbalanced by the sudden shift in weight, it almost toppled backward, and he had to grab the edge of his desk to keep from being pitched to the floor. "I'll be damned," he muttered, shaking his head. "It's a racket. An academic extortion racket."

He'd never heard of anything like this before. It must have come into practice during his sabbatical, along with a newfound touchiness among American college students as a whole. It was a trap that no one had warned him about, and he'd walked straight into it.

"You didn't know this?" Looking up at him again, the girl appeared to be just as astonished as he was.

"Hell, no! I've been gone for the last couple of years." T-Rex pointed to a photo of a radio telescope tacked to the bulletin board above his desk. "There's where I've been… the Wilner Radio Observatory, UNE's dish in the Green Mountain National Forest up in Vermont. I've been coordinating a new SETI operation—"

"SETI… that stands for Search for Extraterrestrial Intelligence, right?" She seemed genuinely interested.

"Yes, but never mind that now." T-Rex impatiently shook his head. "Are you telling me that your classmates were just fishing for A's when they began accusing me of everything that got this on my door?" He stabbed a finger at the swastika.

Her face turned red. "Oh, no. I think Trey… that's the guy who claimed you were homophobic… really was offended. He's very sensitive about people making fun of gays—"

"Even though I'm gay myself?"

"Well, yeah, but… aren't you offended when someone does that, too?"

He slowly let out his breath. "My dear, I've endured far worse. Back when I was your age, if there had been even the slightest hint that I was homosexual, I would have lost my job and might have even been arrested and put in jail. Just as attractive young ladies like you were called co-eds and expected to be cheerleaders, not physics majors."

"I'm not a physics major." She took a seat in the chair beside his desk. "I'm majoring in computer sciences. I just wanted to take Intro to Astro because it sounds cool."

"Well, good for you. You've got an open mind, at least." Despite what she'd done, T-Rex found himself warming up to her. She was the sort of student he liked to find in his class, curious enough about the universe to spend a semester with him. It was too bad she'd never have that chance. "In any case, believe me when I say that there are far worse things than being asked whether you've ever been kissed."

"I'm sorry." Again, her head hung low. "If I'd ever known this was going to happen, I would've never—"

"It's all right." T-Rex hesitated, then reached over to give her hand a gentle squeeze. "That wasn't your intent. I know that now."

Forgiving this girl was tough, but necessary. He knew that it was the only way he'd ever get through the rest of his life without despising the place where he'd spent thirty-three years as a teacher. He was leaving UNE under a cloud, but he didn't want his memories to be overcast by this.

Still, there was a limit to his forgiveness. Perhaps he could let a naïve student off the hook, and he could even absolve the university administration from blame, but others were knowingly responsible for what they'd done. And turning the other cheek wasn't something he was ready to do.

"Thank you." The girl wiped a hand across her eyes. "If there's anything I could do for you, any way I could make things right—"

"Be careful, my dear." With a wary glance out the door to make sure no one had heard her, T-Rex hastily withdrew his hand. "Say that to the wrong faculty member and it could be misinterpreted any number of ways."

Her face became ashen as he said this; she'd just realized what he meant. T-Rex tried not to smile. Despite her earlier bluster about sexism, she was actually rather innocent. "No, my quarrel isn't with you," he went on. "You and your classmates were manipulated by someone else for purposes about which you were unaware. You were simply his tools."

As he spoke, his gaze traveled in the direction of Luis Tuleja's office. She noticed this. "You mean Dr. Tuleja, don't you?" she asked quietly, and he nodded. "I thought so. Just a little while ago, I got email from the registrar's office, announcing that he was taking over your classes from now on. I came down here to see if there was going to be a different syllabus, and when I saw your door open—"

"I understand." This was the first time he'd been here all week; she must have heard him talking to himself. But something she'd happened to mention just a moment ago... "So now you're one of his students, yes?" This wasn't really a question, but she nodded anyway. "And what did you say your major is?"

"Computer sciences."

"I see... I see." Regarding her askance, he absently stroked his beard. "Did you mean what you just said, about wanting to make things right with me?"

"Yes." Again she nodded, her blue eyes solemn. "Yes, I meant it."

He bent forward in his chair. "I really mean this," he said softly, a near whisper that carried no further than his desk. "I've lost my job and my professional standing because of... well, Dr. Tuleja is one, but he's not alone... and I think I'm entitled to some payback. You can help me. Are you willing to do that?"

She seemed to think it over, for only a moment. "Okay," she said quietly, nodding her head. "Sure."

"Very well, then, kick the door shut. And you can start by telling me your name."

MARVIN and the MarsCubes

"Princess?" Dandridge stares at the professor. "You're kidding... her name really *is* Princess?"

"Uh-huh." T-Rex smiles. "Princess Diana Kirby. Her mother was a big fan, and she was born shortly after Di was killed. She doesn't like the name very much—"

"Yeah, I know. A waitress at the diner down the road called her that, and she just about took her head off. I take it that she prefers to go by her middle name."

"No, no, she hates Diana just as much. But she's stuck with that name, too, until she's on her own and her parents have to let her change it to something else." T-Rex scowls. "She's leaning toward Gaga, but I'm trying to talk her out of it."

"Right. So she's a big part of this story, isn't she?"

T-Rex doesn't respond at once, but instead folds his arms across his chest and silently regards the reporter with narrowed eyes. "You want to write her in, too," he says at last, "but I meant what I said about keeping her out of this. Princess did some of the dirty work, and she came with me when I went on the lam, but this whole thing is my idea, not hers."

"So let's talk about that. You mentioned Project MARVIN—"

"Right. Short for Multiband Alien Radio Verification International Network. The syntax is a bit tortured, I admit, but it's a way of paying homage to the old Warner Brothers cartoon character... you know the one."

"Sure. And this was the SETI program you helped establish—"

"'Helped establish,' my ass. MARVIN was my brainchild. If you don't get anything else right in your story, at least get that straight."

"I'll do my best."

"Please do." Ignoring Dandridge's expression, T-Rex goes on. "MARVIN is a global SETI project that's been set up in the northern hemisphere. Seven radio telescopes in all... along with two in California and Vermont, we've also got dishes in Scotland, Romania, Russia, China, and Japan, all located between 40 and 60 degrees North. The observatories operating them have coordinated their computer systems so that, during certain times of day, each dish is aimed to scan a narrow region of the night sky. Each region slightly overlaps the one beside it, so as the Earth turns, the dish there conducts a multiband sweep of the radio spectrum within its assigned area, with each sweep lasting about two hours. At the end of those two hours, it hands off to the neighboring dish to the west, and that one in turn sweeps the adjacent region for another couple of hours before handing off to the next dish, and so on."

"And they've been searching for—?"

"You know that already. Signs of intelligent life beyond the solar system. But MARVIN is unlike any other SETI program that's been done over the last fifty years or so. In nearly all previous searches, going back to Project Ozma in 1960, the assumption was made that aliens would use radio transmitters, and furthermore, they'd be transmitting on a relatively narrow band between 1,420 and 1,667 megahertz... what my mentor Philip Morrison dubbed 'the waterhole' since those are the emission lines of molecular hydrogen and oxygen. But except for anomalies like the so-called 'wow' signal that was picked up by the Ohio State dish in 1977, nothing much has come from watching the waterhole. Even ambitious programs like Project META at the old Harvard-Smithsonian dish didn't produce any verifiable results."

"Got it." Dandridge knows much of this already, but he lets T-Rex ramble on, if only because he wants to get the professor's explanation in his own words.

"Over the last several years, some of us in the SETI community have been questioning the old orthodoxy, wondering if the nature of the transmissions we're trying to find may be different from what we've assumed. Specifically, we've been considering the possibility of 'Benford Beacons' like the ones proposed by brothers Greg and Jim Benford and Jim's son Dominic. The general idea is, since an alien civilization might not be constantly transmitting a waterhole signal because it would cost a great deal of energy to do so, they may instead be sending irregular pulses at higher frequencies… that is, microwave transmissions in the S through X-band range."

"So MARVIN was set up for this kind of search."

"Correct. An organized full-sky sweep conducted over twelve months, utilizing seven dishes in six countries in the northern hemisphere. Since each observatory only has to commit its dish for just a couple of hours each night, the workload is shared. And if a signal is found that fits the parameters of a possible intelligent source, the other observatories can work together to verify whether or not it's the real deal."

"Hence the name."

"Right." T-Rex nods. "The idea was to approach radio observatories south of the equator about establishing another MARVIN down there, where we'd be able to extend the search to stars like Alpha Centauri that can't be seen from the northern hemisphere. But when I came up with MARVIN, I thought there was a better than even chance we'd pick up something in the twelve-month period we'd be sweeping the northern sky."

"And for how long had you been searching when you detected TKA-01… that is, when you *reported* having detected TKA-01?"

"MARVIN was turned on about two weeks before I returned to the university. The scope we're using for the Northeast American sector is the Wilner Radio Observatory in southwestern Vermont. I flipped the switch at the dish myself, then closed up the shack and came home. Aside from an on-site operator who lives nearby, the whole thing is automated, with the search results coming in via satellite link so I could keep an eye on things from my office at the university or even from my house… which, of course, turned out to be rather fortuitous."

"How's that?"

"MARVIN was just half of the scam. The other half was UNE's MarsCube."

"You mentioned it earlier. Something about it being Dr. Tuleja's pet project."

"Oh, yes… and believe me, it was a real pleasure to use it to my own advantage." A cunning smile spreads across T-Rex's face. "Luis never had a clue that I'd hoisted him by his own petard… or probe, as the case may be."

The smile fades. He stops to look away again, as if mulling over his next words. "Perhaps it's best if I let Princess speak for herself," he says at last, "if only because she's more familiar with the technical details than I am. But—"

He bends forward, this time to look Dandridge straight in the eye. "Look, I'm serious about keeping her name out of this," T-Rex says, pointing a finger at the journalist. "I want you to promise me that you'll treat her as an anonymous source, okay?"

"I can't promise you anything," Dandridge replies, "particularly if she's a key participant. But I'll keep in mind that you don't want her to be identified by name, and I'll do my best to do so."

T-Rex hesitates, then picks up the room phone from the bedside table and taps three digits. "Can you come over?" he says a few seconds later. "He wants to talk to you." A pause, then he hangs up. "She's on her way."

A minute goes by, then Princess lets herself in with a keycard T-Rex has apparently given her. She's already dressed for bed: a white tank top and blue jammie bottoms with the Wonder Woman logo across the rear, looking like every frat boy's favorite fantasy.

"Wanna talk to me about something?" Princess slides past Dandridge without looking at him. Taking her place at the head of the bed, she puts her back against the wall, curls her legs beneath her, and hugs a pillow against her chest as if it were a shield.

"Uh-huh." T-Rex nods toward Dandridge. "I want you to help me explain about how we hijacked MarsCube 4."

"Really?" Her face lights up with a happy smile. "Awesome!"

The Conspirators

T-Rex was just finishing up in the kitchen when he spotted headlights coming down the drive. He took a moment to move a pot to the warmer plate, then picked up a terrycloth towel and, wiping his hands on it, walked to the kitchen door. He watched as a Subaru hatchback reached the end of the dirt road leading to his house. It paused for a few moments, as if the driver was trying to decide whether this lonely cottage out in the woods was indeed the place she was supposed to be going. T-Rex stepped out onto the porch and waved, and the Subie resumed its motion, sliding in alongside his Jeep Cherokee.

It was a pleasant autumn evening, just cool enough to be comfortable, scented with fallen leaves and dying wildflowers. He held open the door to air out the kitchen, which was overheated and smelled of fish, as he waited for his dinner guest. The Subaru's dome light flashed on, momentarily revealing Princess as she climbed out. She slammed the car door shut and, with a somewhat wary glance about her surroundings, walked up the gravel path to the porch stairs.

"Right on time." T-Rex beamed at her as she marched up the stairs. "Have trouble finding the place?"

"Naw. Got Google Map on my phone… took me right here." She wore a woolen fisherman's sweater, a denim jacket, and suede knee boots, and had pulled her hair back in a French braid. She paused at the top of the stairs to look around again from the porch. Woods surrounded them, with the lights of the nearest neighbor just a glimmer in the darkness. "Really live out in the sticks, don't you?"

"The house dates back to the last century. Bought it cheap thirty years ago and fixed it up. Yeah, I like privacy." T-Rex didn't mention the reasons why. Besides the fact that he adored old houses in general, he'd still been sexually active at the time, sometimes bringing home male students whom he'd recognized as being members of the family. He hadn't been kidding when he'd told her that, in the old days, homosexuality would have been grounds for dismissal from the UNE faculty. Having affairs with students would have assured this. So an isolated house on the outskirts of Easthampton meant that he wouldn't have nosy neighbors, and the quiet was worth the daily commute to campus... or at least up until a couple of weeks ago.

Princess nodded as he stepped aside to let her pass. As customary in New England households, the side door was the de facto front door, so the kitchen was the first thing she saw. His was cozy and charming in a masculine sort of way, but not big enough for two people to stand around and chat. "Please, make yourself at home," he said, leading her through the kitchen into the slightly larger dining room where he'd already set the table. "All I have to do is move everything from the kitchen into here, and we'll be ready."

"Awesome." She was already removing her jacket. Admiring the vintage Peter Max print framed on the wall above the antique sideboard, she added, "Cool hippie art."

T-Rex tried not to laugh. What she didn't know would never hurt her. Besides, he had another matter on his mind. "Thanks. Oh, by the way... you didn't tell anyone you were coming out here tonight, did you? Or that you've had any contact with me?"

"No." Still gazing at the print, she shook her head. "Didn't tell anyone, Professor—"

"You can call me Ted. Or T-Rex, if you prefer."

She hesitated. "I like Professor," she said. "Calling you by your first name... I dunno, it just doesn't feel right. Do you mind?"

"Not at all." In fact, he was complimented. He knew exactly where she was coming from. Philip Morrison had invited him to call him Phil, but he'd never been able to bring himself to address him as anything but Dr. Morrison. "Good. We need to keep all this a secret, and that means no one must know that you're seeing me. Not your roommate, not your boyfriend—"

"My roommate and I don't really get along, and I broke up with my boyfriend a few months ago." Arms folded across her chest, she drifted from the dining room into the den. "And no offense, Professor, but if anyone at school knew I was here right now, they'd run me off campus. You're not Mr. Popular, y'know. Everyone thinks it was a major victory that you were fired."

"Retired... but that's okay. Let 'em believe what they want." He was relieved to learn that she hadn't told anyone about him; for what he was planning, secrecy was paramount. "Go ahead and look around," he said as he returned to the kitchen. "Dinner will be on the table in just a few minutes."

T-Rex had taken a chance with the menu for the evening. When he'd emailed Princess to invite her to dinner, he'd neglected to ask what she'd like to eat. So he'd pretended to be feeding a lovely young boy instead, just as he once had in happier times, and prepared the sort of meal she wasn't going to find in the student cafeteria: grilled salmon with a raspberry marinade, garlic mashed potatoes, steamed asparagus with homemade Hollandaise sauce, and fresh-baked popovers from a recipe he'd swiped from Judy's in Amherst. T-Rex was nothing if not a good cook; he would've made someone a fine husband, if only marriage had been an option when he was still an eligible bachelor.

He'd also bought a couple of bottles of wine, a tasty Bordeaux appropriate for salmon. He'd done this just as knowingly as he'd planned a dinner that was something other than pizza, tacos, or whatever else she was getting in studentland. Princess might not yet be twenty-one, but he had little doubt that she was no stranger to alcohol. Tonight, though, she wasn't drinking keg beer out of a plastic cup, but the vine from which seduction is made.

And while he had no intentions of luring her into his bed, seducing her was indeed tonight's goal.

His efforts weren't wasted. Princess's eyes widened as he brought the serving platters to the table, and he couldn't help but notice that her hands trembled a little as she spread a linen napkin across her lap. Acting as if the meal hadn't been any trouble at all, T-Rex carefully delivered the salmon filets to both of their plates, then poured her a glass of red wine... not so much as to make it obvious that he wanted to get her just a bit buzzed, but neither did he defer to her age. If necessary, he could always drive her home.

Over dinner, they talked. Not about what he really wanted to discuss; that would come later. Instead, he steered the conversation toward the subject undergrads love to talk about the most: themselves. At first, he did this only to help Princess feel at ease, for she was clearly nervous about being here, but as she went on, he found himself becoming interested. She was from a small town in upstate New York, the sort of upscale Hudson River community where Wall Street financiers like her father relocate their families after making money in the city. He'd run off with another stockbroker a few years ago, though, leaving Princess with her mother, a second-tier fantasy writer who churned out books about magic cats who fight epic wars with dragons.

Princess didn't seem to like either of her parents very much. Like many of her generation, she'd begun using Mom's computer as soon as she could reach the keyboard. Her fascination with the digital world—did anyone call it cyberspace anymore, he wondered, or was that an eighties thing?—was deeper than most, and by the time she got out of high school, she'd decided that she wanted to spend her life in this place. UNE's computer sciences department was just the first step.

As T-Rex listened to Princess Diana Kirby talk about her dreams and aspirations, he couldn't help but marvel at her self-confidence. No, not self-confidence. It went far beyond that, a strange combination of naïveté and adolescent arrogance. At eighteen, she'd already figured out how her life would unfold. Invent a killer ap—an addictive time-waster like Angry Birds, perhaps, or maybe something more useful, like a locator for smoothies—and use it to become wealthy before her twenty-first birthday. Move to some hip city like Boston, Burlington, or Baltimore—all the best cities begin with B—and start her own dot com ("Silicon Valley is so *over*"). Marry an actor or a rock star (she hadn't decided which one yet) and get her picture on the cover of *Wired*. Have her own designer brand of something.

Wealth. Fame. Happiness. Nothing else was remotely possible. Her mother may have named her in fond memory of a member of the British royalty, but Ms. Kirby's daughter really was a princess. She'd been told a long time ago that she was special, and she'd believed it.

T-Rex should have hated her. She was the embodiment of every self-absorbed, air-headed thing he'd lately come to despise about the millennials. But he didn't. To use her generation's favorite expression, in the way that it was meant to be used, she was awesome.

And she was exactly the person he needed to enact his vengeance.

"Well, now," he said once she finally ran out of steam, "that's really quite interesting."

"Really?" She raised her head from locally-made maple froyo he'd put before her as dessert. "I kinda thought... y'know... I might have been babbling a bit much. Maybe boring you."

"Oh, no, not at all. It's good to see a young person like yourself with such ambitions. And I'm sure you have the talent to pull it off." She smiled and nodded, a drop of frozen yogurt dribbling down her chin, accepting her due. "But I wonder..." He trailed off, deliberately looking away to let the uncompleted thought hover between them.

"Wonder what?" she asked, taking the bait.

"Well... if you'd like to do something that would really make you famous. I don't just mean getting into computer magazines and stuff like that, but world famous. Cover of *Time*, front page of the *Boston Globe*—" he was drawing a blank look from her "—maybe even Gizmodo."

Now he had her interest. "Go on."

T-Rex pushed back his chair. "Did you do what I asked you to do, and read up on Project MARVIN? And also the MarsCube the university launched earlier this year?"

"I know about MARVIN," she said, "but I didn't get to the MarsCube thing. Sorry. I've had a ton of homework this week."

"That's okay." He held up a placating hand as he rose from his seat. After a meal this big, he usually liked to sleep it off. Instead, he picked up his wine. "I can explain it just as well as anyone else. Pour yourself another drink, my dear, and follow me to the den."

T-Rex lumbered into the next room, the girl a few steps behind him. This was his favorite part of the house, a cozy, wood-paneled room with Indian carpets on the floor and stained glass in the transom windows, furnished with antiques he'd picked up at shops around Western Massachusetts. From a bookcase stuffed with vintage mystery novels, he picked up a small plastic model on a display stand.

"Do you know what this is?" he asked, handing it to her.

Princess turned the model around in her hand. It was a rectangular cube wrapped in silver-blue Mylar, with solar panels jutting out from each side, a smaller dish antenna protruding from the bottom, and camera lenses in the opposite side. "A MarsCube?"

"That's correct. It's a MarsCube... MarsCube 4, to be exact." T-Rex tapped a finger against the model. "Everyone on the physics faculty received one of these as a souvenir when it was launched last spring. The real one isn't much larger." He held his hands a couple of feet apart. "About the size of a toaster oven, or a stereo system once the solar panels have been deployed."

"Cute."

"Isn't it? And useful, too. They're larger versions of the CubeSats NASA introduced a few years ago, miniature satellites that can be built and launched on a shoestring. Big communications or weather satellites can cost hundreds of millions of dollars, while CubeSats can be built for just a few hundred thousand."

"I take it they're meant to go to Mars."

"Right-o." T-Rex took the model back from her and returned it to the shelf. "A few years ago, a consortium of colleges and universities, including UNE, teamed up with NASA and SpaceX to create a research program intended to spark student interest in space exploration. The six schools that were involved with this designed and built a half-dozen MarsCubes, each with its own particular purpose, comprising sort of a low-cost swarm of Mars probes. Each cube cost about $1 million to develop, build, and launch... dirt cheap for this sort of thing... and last March all six were launched from the Cape aboard a SpaceX rocket and sent on their way to Mars on a low-energy trajectory, with an ETA of about seven months from now."

"And MarsCube 4 was the one from our school."

"Uh-huh. And the faculty member who was in charge of the program was my dear friend Luis Tuleja."

"Sounds exciting." Princess took a sip of wine. T-Rex noted that she was relaxed to the point where she was a little unsteady on her feet, but not so much that her voice was slurred. Good. That's how he wanted her: suggestible, but not drunk.

"Yeah, well..." He shrugged. "I'd be happier if Luis hadn't used it to play campus politics. It's the sort of flashy, high-profile academic project that the administration and trustees love."

"I heard that he took a lot of students down to Florida to watch it lift off."

"He did. He got the university to pay for everyone who'd participated in building MarsCube 4 to go down to Cape Canaveral to watch the launch. And since it so happened that this coincided with spring break, after the launch everyone went down to Cocoa Beach for a—" a sarcastic cough "—scientific colloquium."

"And you think he got everyone on his side?"

"What do you think?" T-Rex walked over to the couch and sat down heavily. "Even before I delivered that lecture, Luis was positioning himself to jump ahead of me for Dr. McCabe's job when she retires… which is ironic, because I really didn't care about getting it anyway. He'd built a lot of support among the students, so when I said those things in class that got you and everyone else so upset—"

"I said I was sorry."

"I know, and I forgive you. But you played right into his hands, gave him an opportunity to have me terminated." He looked straight at her. "So you owe me, kiddo. I like you, but really, you owe me."

Princess nodded as she took a seat at the other end of the couch. "Okay. So what is it that you want to do?"

"I want to get back at that bastard," T-Rex said. "But more importantly, I want to make a point about the social media and how people use it to twist facts and blow things out of proportion. An object lesson, if you will… one that no one will be able to ignore."

"What do you got in mind?"

He smiled. "We're going to hack MarsCube 4," he replied. "And once we've done that, we're going use it and MARVIN to perpetuate the biggest scientific hoax of all time."

"Awesome."

Freshman Fatale

Like most pretty girls, Princess had become aware early in life of the effect her looks had on males. As early as kindergarten, boys were trying to kiss her, and by the time she reached puberty she'd developed the usual range of feminine defenses against unwanted sexual attention. Nonetheless, it came as a surprise to find herself being coveted by men as old as her father. She'd been raised to respect and obey her elders, so it was a little surprising to find that she had to learn how to deal with the less overt and more sophisticated kind of approach a young lady might expect to receive from a man twice her age.

It was tiresome. Indeed, there were times that Princess found herself wishing that her looks weren't as perfect as they were. It would have been nice if nature had given her something to mitigate them a bit: buck teeth, maybe, or a big nose. Even a flat chest or smaller hips would have been appreciated. But Mom had been easy on the eyes and Dad was handsome, and their genes were responsible for a child who'd always have men imaging what she'd be like in bed. If there was any advantage to her looks, it was the same one every beautiful woman since Cleopatra had learned: it was easy for her to manipulate men.

Case in point: Luis Tuleja.

On the Tuesday afternoon following dinner with Dr. Reggs, Princess showed up for her appointment with Dr. Tuleja. She'd emailed her new Astronomy 101 instructor the day before, requesting a meeting with him to discuss some problems she was having with the material he'd recently covered in his lectures. He'd scheduled her for 2:45 P.M., with the usual request that she arrive promptly and give him plenty of advance notice if she had to cancel.

The last thing Princess intended to do was cancel this meeting.

That morning, she chose her outfit with care. Keeping in mind that the days were becoming cooler and they were already past Indian summer (or "Indigenous American People's Summer," which she'd lately learned was the more culturally sensitive term), she decided that a tank top and shorts would be inappropriate. On the other hand, a pair of Levi's skinny jeans —faded blue, pre-ripped down the leg, tight as a second skin—together with a black cashmere V-neck sweater and high-heel boots gave her the look she wanted: sexy, but with just enough restraint that she didn't look like a total slut.

She contemplated not wearing a bra, but instead decided to go for broke and use her secret weapon: a wonder bra from Victoria's Secret, black lace and nearly as small as a bikini top, but nonetheless fitted to lift and separate. She put on the low-cut sweater, examined herself in the dorm mirror, and smiled. Perfect. You could have bounced a penny off her sternum and it would have fallen straight between her breasts.

"Dressing up today, aren't you, Di?" Sitting cross-legged on her bed, her roommate peered at her over the top of the Harry Potter book she was reading.

"A little." Princess made a half-turn to look at her butt. That area of her anatomy wasn't so bad either. But it was the chest that mattered.

"New guy?" A half-smile of feigned interest. Faun read a lot; whenever she was back in their dorm room, there was almost always a book in her hands. However, everything she read seemed to be a kids' fantasy novel: Rick Riordan, Tamora Pierce, Catherine Valente, J.K. Rowling, even the ones Princess's mother had written. When she wasn't reading, she was using her crayons on the stack of coloring books beside her bed. Princess figured that Faun might one day try a book meant for adults.

"You could say that." A glance at the clock on her desk told her that her first class was in twenty minutes. She grabbed her backpack and headed for the door. "Later."

Princess knew her outfit was having its desired effect because she went through the day receiving appreciative second-takes from nearly every guy she encountered, and a few girls as well. UNE had more than its share of desirable young women; *Playboy* and *Maxim* had been known to send their scouts to the university in search of fresh meat for their readers. Now it was her turn. Princess didn't normally dress this way, but she certainly knew how to set the bait. And today, she was a man trap.

Her second class was Astronomy 101. For the past couple of weeks, ever since the infamous lecture that had cost Dr. Reggs his job, Princess had taken to sitting in the back of the lecture hall. Although many of her classmates considered her to be a hero for her role in the affair, she was embarrassed by what she'd done. Today, she returned to her former seat at the front of the room, where she could be easily seen from the podium. And when Dr. Tuleja arrived to deliver today's lecture, she was waiting for him.

Princess had to admit, she admired his dedication to his work. It took nearly fifteen minutes for Luis Tuleja to notice the female student in the second row whose eyes seemed to follow his every move. But once he did, Princess had him hooked. Unlike his predecessor, Dr. Tuleja was an animated speaker. Using a wireless lapel mike and a handheld remote to free himself from the podium, he paced back and forth across the stage, changing the Hubble deep-space images on the screen behind him as he spoke about the revolution in astronomy brought on by orbital telescopes. And every time he looked at the audience, he found Princess watching him, legs crossed and bent forward just slightly, a faint smile on her lips. She knew that she'd had an effect on him when he faltered at one point and had to return to the podium to check his lecture notes.

This was probably the first time he'd ever noticed this particular student. And she'd made sure that he'd remember her a few hours later.

When the time came for her appointment with him, Princess arrived ten minutes early. As usual, there was a short line of students waiting in the hall outside his office. A week ago, he'd moved down and across the hall to take over the office formerly occupied by his departed colleague. It had a nicer view from the window. He'd had the door refinished, and even managed to keep the furniture.

Knowing that she'd need more than the fifteen minutes allotted to her, Princess had a quick, whispered conservation with the freshman standing next in line. Elvis had a hard time getting girls to notice him, so when a gorgeous blonde begged him to swap places with her in line so she could get to an appointment in time, he was only too happy to do so. In a minute, another student walked out of Dr.Tuleja's office, and Princess walked in.

"Hi, Dr. Tuleja," she said, holding out her hand. "I'm Diana."

She almost never used her middle name, which she disliked nearly as much as Princess, but it seemed a little more intimate for him to call her that than the nickname everyone else used. On the other hand, she could have said that her name was Mary Jo Grunt and it wouldn't have made any difference. Tuleja's eyes lit up when he saw her; he'd obviously recognized her as the lovely young thing from his lecture earlier that day.

"Hello... um, Diana." A glance at his schedule book confirmed that she wasn't the student he'd been expecting to see next, but he didn't make an issue of it. As he rose to take her hand, Princess noted that he'd been sitting in T-Rex's old doctor's chair. Apparently Tuleja managed to lay claim to his trophy before the university removed the rest of the professor's belongings.

However, the room hadn't been rearranged. The desk was where it had been a few weeks ago, with the bulletin board just above it. When she took a seat in the straight-back wooden chair beside the desk, she saw that the professor was right: she could easily see and read everything pinned to the cork board.

All she had to do was get him to not notice the direction in which she was looking.

"Thank you for seeing me," she said, bending forward a little to deposit her pack on the floor. "I'm really *so* sorry to bother you, but I'm having a little trouble understanding something you said in class last week."

"Not at all. Not at all." As he spoke, Luis Tuleja's gaze traveled to her décolletage. And that was when Princess knew that the rest would be almost childishly easy.

Space Hack

Three days later, Princess walked into a Pizza Barn on Route 10 just outside Springfield. She didn't look anything like the way she had when she'd had her meeting with Luis Tuleja; today, she wore old jeans and a hoodie. She stood for a few moments at the front counter, pretending to study the menu board while surreptitiously scanning the dining room from beneath her sweatshirt's raised hood.

The place was almost empty. As expected, she recognized no one among the small handful of customers. It was well past the lunch hour, and this particular Pizza Barn was far enough away from campus that it was unlikely she'd spot anyone who might recognize her. T-Rex had cautioned her that it was important that she needed to find a place where she'd be anonymous. If something went wrong…

No. Nothing was going to go wrong, for now she was no longer Princess Diana Kirby, but DarkskyStarkiller, the most dangerous mercenary in the galaxy. And DarkskyStarkiller was on a mission of vengeance and could not be stopped.

DarkskyStarkiller ordered a six-inch Italian grinder with no onions, picked up a bag of Doritos, and poured a Sierra Mist from the soda dispenser, then found a table in the corner where she was away from the few other people in the dining room. She opened her daypack and pulled out her Dell laptop, then logged onto the restaurant's customer server. Princess had picked Pizza Barn because they offered free WiFi, and once she connected to the Internet through their server using the PGP-generated logon she normally used for gaming—DarkskyStarkiller was a frequent player in the Galaxy Patrol online game—she was virtually untraceable. Even if she screwed up and gave someone reason to back-track her movements, the trail would end at a pizza joint in Western Massachusetts, not her dorm room or anywhere else on the UNE campus.

Princess waited until her sandwich came before she reached into her jeans and pulled out a thumb drive. A bite from her sandwich, then she plugged the drive into the serial port. Once the program contained on it was booted up, she accessed the public-access portal of UNet, UNE's campus computer network.

As she worked, pausing every now and then to nibble at her grinder and chips, Princess reflected on how easy it had been to gain access to MarsCube 4's control system. T-Rex had overestimated the difficulty; he thought they'd have to sleaze their way into NASA's Deep Space Network at the Jet Propulsion Lab in Pasadena, California, which would have been a very difficult hack indeed, probably beyond her abilities. But once she investigated further, Princess discovered that it wouldn't be necessary to get anywhere near JPL. Because each MarsCube was designed to have independent controls accessible by the teachers and students who'd designed and built them, all she needed to do was access it through UNet. She could do that from any public WiFi; once she was on UNet, all she needed was a password other than her own to gain entry to the university's myriad departmental computer systems... and she'd gained that by a social visit to an upperclassmen in her dorm who wanted to sleep with her. It's amazing what you can find on someone's desk after you send him out for beer.

She was even more surprised—shocked, really—to find that any further security walls around MarsCube 4 were virtually non-existent. Apparently neither Luis nor his students had seriously considered the notion that anyone would want to hack into their space probe. One more password was all they needed to get in, and that was easy enough to learn.

Just as T-Rex suspected, Luis had written down the password and pinned it to the bulletin board above his desk. Like most eggheads, Luis had a bad memory for trivialities such as this, and it was a weakness that T-Rex and Princess were able to exploit. So while Luis was checking out her breasts during her visit to his office—Princess wondered what his wife would think if she knew the way he was ogling his female students—she was checking out the Post-it notes on the bulletin board.

And there it was: *Myprobe1*. How cryptic.

That evening, she'd brought what she learned over to Dr. Reggs's house, where they logged onto UNet and took their first look at the MarsCube operating system. They were amused to discover, despite all the hype, just how primitive it actually was. All the probe was meant to do was to fly past Mars, point its camera at the planet, take some pictures, and transmit the images back to Earth. Whoopie. As T-Rex disdainfully pointed out, Mariner 9 had done pretty much the same thing almost fifty years ago. MarsCube 4 had as much to do with planetary research as an Estes rocket does with space technology. Its purpose, really, was to make the students who'd built it look good and raise Luis Tuleja's status in the physics department.

But...

But the MarsCubes had a more sophisticated communication system than those aboard the NASA spacecraft of previous generations. The MarsCubes used SDR (software defined radio) transmitters. Smaller and mass-conservative, they sent back their messages via X-band microwave transmitters instead of the older UHF radios that required larger antennas. Furthermore, ground controllers could change the software en route without any hardware upgrades. As it turned out, MarsCube 4's SDR software utilized a source code that was ridiculously easy to locate. One of Tuleja's students had apparently decided to score geek bragging rights by publishing it on a web site for open-source software, which was where Princess found it.

Once Princess downloaded the code, she and T-Rex closely studied MarsCube 4's computer program, and then made slight but significant alterations to suit their purposes. All she needed to do now was to load the changeling software into the MarsCube 4 control system on UNet. The university's server would automatically connect with NASA's Deep Space Network at JPL, which in turn would transmit the program to the probe itself.

DarkskyStarkiller took a few minutes to finish her grinder while she scrolled down her screen, reviewing the program she and T-Rex had laboriously written over the course of a weekend at his house. Satisfied that there were no missing symbols or code junk that might screw things up, she daintily wiped her mouth with a paper napkin, took a slug from her soda, then rested her fingers on the keyboard.

"Torpedoes armed and targeted," she murmured. "Fire." And then she tapped the *Enter* key.

Princess waited a minute to make sure that the program had successfully uploaded, then she exited UNet, disengaged and removed the thumb drive, and shut down her laptop. Although she tried to remain calm, deep inside she felt her heart hammering against her chest. Although she knew that it was highly unlikely that an investigation—if there even was one—would lead anyone here, she hastily returned the Dell to her backpack and left the booth. The thumb drive and the remains of her lunch went into the trash barrel as she hurried out the door.

Fifteen minutes later, Princess parked her Subaru in the student lot beside her dorm. Her next class was in about a half-hour; she could have gone straight there, but by then she'd calmed down. There were no cop cars in hot pursuit, no men in black suits and shades waiting for her to show up. And she was curious... had anyone noticed what she'd just done?

The Goddard building was on the way to class. She decided to drop in, just to see what she could see.

When she reached the second floor, she immediately noticed a small knot of students outside Dr. Tuleja's office. There were always students waiting to see him, but this time was different. As Princess walked closer, she saw the expressions of alarm and confusion on their faces. The office door was shut, but nonetheless everyone could hear Tuleja's angry voice coming through:

"*Mierda! Malditasonda!*"

Princess sidled up beside Dylan, a boy she knew from the Astronomy 101 class that Dr. Tuleja had taken over following T-Rex's departure. "What's going on?" she asked.

"I dunno," Dylan murmured, "but he's wicked pissed."

Another classmate, Lennon, looked over his shoulder at them. "They lost contact with the Mars probe," he said quietly. "It happened—"

"*NASA de mierda!*" Something crashed inside the office as if an object had been thrown against the wall, followed by a string of ugly-sounding Spanish.

"I was in his office when the phone rang," Lennon went on, lowering his voice although there was little chance the professor would hear him. "It was JPL, telling him that the MarsCube has gone dark. He dropped everything and went into UNet, but—" he shrugged "—he got nothing. Probe's dead."

"Sucks," Dylan said.

"Way," Lennon replied.

"Dude," Princess agreed.

She continued down the hall until she reached the emergency exit. Looking both ways to make sure no one had spotted her, she pushed open the door. It made no noise as she opened it; a handful of cigarette butts beside the stairwell showed where someone had disabled the fire alarm to turn this place into a smoker's den. Anyway, the stairway was deserted. So long as no one had a nic fit in the next few minutes, she was fine.

She pulled out her iPhone and called T-Rex. He answered on the third ring. *"Yes, Your Majesty?"*

She smiled. He'd lately begun calling her that. She wouldn't have tolerated this from anyone else, but from him… "It's done, Professor."

"Excellent. Well done." A pause. *"You wouldn't by chance know whether Luis is aware of what happened, do you?"*

"Yeah, I do. And yeah, he is."

His rose expectantly: *"And—?"*

"I don't know Spanish, but it sounds like he's real pissed."

A gleeful laugh, and from the other end the sound of a hand slapping down on a table. *"Yes! Yes, yes, yes! Take that, you backstabbing bastard!"*

Despite her anxiety, Princess giggled. Suddenly, she was much less nervous than she'd been a few minutes ago. "Glad you're happy, Professor."

"Deliriously, Your Highness."

"So what do we do now?"

"First, come over tonight for dinner so we can celebrate with a bottle of wine. Can you do that?"

"Sure. Love to." There was a boy in her dorm who'd been bugging her about going out. He was cute and all that, but somehow she preferred Dr. Reggs's company. With him, she'd never have to worry about clumsy passes and misinterpreted signals. She could dance in front of him in her underwear and he'd probably just warn her about catching a cold. "Is that it?"

"For the time being, yes." His tone became serious. *"Now, we wait."*

The Great Galactic Ghoul

"So what then?" Dandridge asks.

T-Rex raises an eyebrow. "You mean, what did we do after we killed MarsCube 4? Why, we went to Disneyworld."

"No, we didn't," Princess says. "Why would we do that? I've been there. It sucks."

T-Rex casts a querulous look in her direction; she reacts with a blank expression that confirms that she didn't get the professor's joke. T-Rex quietly snorts and shakes his head, then looks at Dandridge again.

"We didn't jump up and down cheering, if that's what you mean," he goes on. "Even if the probe was Luis Tuleja's pride and joy, the fact remained that it was an expensive scientific instrument, albeit of only limited usefulness. Rendering it inoperative wasn't something I enjoyed—"

"Oh, c'mon," Princess says. "You got drunk that night. You even went out and howled at the moon."

"Well, all right, maybe I enjoyed it just a *little*." T-Rex holds up a thumb and forefinger just a half-inch apart. "But knocking it out of contact with JPL wasn't the point of what we were doing, even if it did take a lot of wind out of Luis's sails. The point was to give everyone the illusion that MarsCube 4 had been lost en route to Mars... which, of course, was something that everyone kinda half-expected anyway, even if no one was saying so aloud."

"Why is that?" Dandridge asks.

"Look at the history of unmanned space exploration. About two-thirds of the probes America, Europe, and Russia have sent to Mars over the last fifty years or so have failed. They've blown up shortly after launch, or lost radio contact for reasons unknown, or sailed past the planet without achieving orbit, or crashed while attempting landing, or any of a number of different things. Back in the '60s, the failure record was so bad that someone at NASA even came up with a mythical culprit... the Great Galactic Ghoul, the invisible monster that lurks somewhere between Earth and Mars and eats poor wayward space probes."

Dandridge smiles. "I think I've heard of that, yeah."

"So you'd understand why no one except maybe Luis and his students were greatly surprised when contact was lost with MarsCube 4. They figured the Ghoul got it. In fact, that's why the mission planners decided to launch six MarsCubes in the first place. They expected at least one or two wouldn't make it to their destination, so they compensated with design redundancy... and as it just so happened, it was the one that UNE built that the Ghoul picked for his latest snack."

"I was in his class when Dr. Tuleja made the announcement the next day," Princess says. "You could tell he was really shook up about it."

"And how did you feel?" Dandridge asks. "You were responsible, after all."

Princess shrugs. "I guess I felt a little guilty. And I was still afraid that NASA or someone would catch on, even though I'd made really sure that they couldn't trace it back to me." She looks at T-Rex again. "But then I remembered what he'd done to the professor and figured that, y'know, maybe he deserved it."

Dandridge says nothing, but nonetheless he marvels at the young lady sitting on the bed. On one hand, it's obvious that she's come to care deeply about the older man whose teaching career she'd inadvertently ended with what was meant to be little more than a campus prank. On the other hand, though, she appears to have no qualms about wrecking the work of another professor and his students as an act of revenge. Princess Diana Kirby has a very strange sense of morality. For the life of him, he can't decide if it comes from her individual personality, or something shared by her generation as a whole.

"At any rate," T-Rex goes on, "once everyone gave up the probe for lost, it gave us time to work out the rest of our plan. Because taking down the cube was just the first step."

"Yeah, uh-huh." Warming to the subject, Princess tosses aside the pillow and sits forward. "See, we still had control of the probe. And once the professor worked out the algorithms for its probable trajectory, we had a fix on its location between Earth and Mars, even if the university or NASA didn't. So we always knew that, when the time came, we could get back in touch with it."

"We didn't just sit on our hands for the next three months," T-Rex says. "We were quietly working together on the rest of the scheme… and I do mean quietly, because our first rule was to avoid the phone from now on and exchange email only when necessary."

"And even then," Princess adds, "we worked out certain protocols for sharing data, like making sure that we used PGP encryption at all times. PGP means—"

"Pretty Good Privacy. I know." Dandridge is tempted to tell Princess that he was working with computers when she was playing with Barbie dolls.

"We did most of the work at my house," T-Rex says. "She'd come over Friday or Saturday evening, I'd fix us a nice dinner, and then we'd spend the rest of the night in my study working on our little project."

"And no one knew?"

"Nope," Princess says, then adds, "well, my roommate kinda did." There's an alarmed expression on T-Rex's face as he looks at her, and she giggles. "Faun asked me where I was going every weekend, and I told her that I was spending the night with an older man."

"Well, at least you weren't lying," T-Rex says with a wry smile, then he turns to Dandridge again. "We finished our work just before the semester ended. We broke for her to take her finals and go home for the holidays—"

"Always a lot of fun, let me tell you." Princess sighs. "After two weeks of hearing about my mother's cats and dragons and getting calls from my old boyfriend because he can't get laid at Yale, I couldn't wait to get back for the January mid-term."

"She came back just after New Year's," T-Rex says, "and then we were ready to go."

Mountain Jam

Winter came late to Southern Vermont that year. The first snow more than a couple of inches deep didn't fall on the region until after the holidays, giving local residents their first brown Christmas in recent memory. But the bars in Brattleboro had barely put away their New Year's Eve decorations when a nor'easter rolled in, the first of the season. A day later, the entire state lay beneath a cold white blanket.

A soft and gentle snow was falling as the eight-year-old Jeep Cherokee pulled off Route 7 and headed up a narrow road leading into hill country a few miles east of the highway. Only a few houses and farms lay close to the road. The winter sun had just begun to set, casting a dull luminescence across the thick grey clouds to the west. The Jeep's headlights flashed on, and as they did a large wooden road sign briefly became visible: *Entering Green Mountains National Forest.*

Past the sign, the dwellings abruptly vanished, replaced by dense woodlands sloping upward toward white-capped mountain ranges. There were no other cars on the road, which was already being coated by a thin skein of fresh powder. The Jeep's headlights revealed snowflakes like a swarm of tiny comets falling through space. Evening comes early in New England during the first month of the year; although it was still late afternoon, already it seemed like nightfall.

Inside the Jeep, T-Rex turned down the Broadway show tunes with which he'd been torturing Princess—she's already threatened to cut his throat and bury his body in a shallow grave if he ever again played the *Fiddler on the Roof* soundtrack in her presence—and reached for the smartphone attached to a hands-free bracket on the dashboard. "Quiet now," he said as he pushed a number in the phone's directory. "Time to make sure Robbie's still on vacation."

Princess said nothing as she hugged herself closer. The Jeep's heater didn't work well enough to keep her as warm as she would've liked, and although T-Rex had obliged her by stopping for coffee a couple of times on the way up from Springfield, her parka and mittens weren't quite keeping the January chill at bay. So she listened quietly as the phone burred six times, then an unfamiliar voice came on the line:

"*You've reached the Wilner Radio Observatory of the University of New England,*" a pleasant male voice said from the phone. "*No one is present to take your call just now, but if you'd care to leave a message—*"

"Excellent." T-Rex ended the call and returned both hands to the wheel. "Just as I expected... Robbie's still in Florida."

"Who's Robbie, and why is he so lucky?"

"Robbie Dollens, the on-site operator. We'll pass his house in just a few minutes. He's a postgrad fellow working on his doctoral dissertation. He pays his tuition by minding the dish. Been doing it for some time now, which means the university gets a good deal from him. He—"

"So why is it so important that he's in Florida?"

"Because I don't want anyone knowing we're here." T-Rex sighed as if explaining the obvious. "Every year, right after Christmas, he and his wife go down to Fort Myers for a couple of weeks, so I was counting on him still being gone when we arrived." He smiled. "Unless a ranger or a moose happens to drop in, we're all by ourselves."

"Awesome. Keep that in mind before you put on *Man of La Mancha* again."

The road continued uphill until it reached a fork at the top of a low ridge, with the right turn becoming an unpaved road leading downhill and deeper into the forest. T-Rex took the turn without hesitation, shifting into four-wheel drive and switching on the high beams so they could penetrate the snow falling through the trees. The road reached the bottom of the slope, where a creek cut through a mountain valley between the surrounding mountains. The Jeep crossed an old trestle bridge; about a half-mile further down, they passed a two-story New England saltbox on the left side of the road, the first house they'd seen since entering federal land. A small signpost beside the driveway read *Dollens*. Aside from some Christmas lights in the windows, the place was dark, the doors of its attached garage lowered.

All of a sudden, they came upon an eight-foot chain-link fence, its locked gate dully reflecting the headlight beams. On the other side of the gate, a giant steel dish loomed out of the snow-flecked darkness like an immense spider's web woven by some monstrous arachnid lurking in the valley.

A steerable Cassegrain radio telescope eighty-four feet in diameter, the Wilner Radio Observatory originally belonged to NASA's orbital tracking network during the Mercury, Gemini, and Apollo programs of the '60s and '70s. Following the Apollo-Soyuz mission in 1975, NASA sold the dish to the University of New England, where it was renamed for the astronomy professor T-Rex eventually replaced and refitted for its new role as a research tool. It seemed out of place in this little gully between mountain ridges, but that was precisely the point for its location. The surrounding mountains of the national forest shielded the dish from most forms of man-made electromagnetic radiation, giving it a radio-quiet zone for it to conduct its observations of the heavens. A perfect listening post for signs of extraterrestrial intelligence.

T-Rex pulled to a stop in front of the gate, then reached into his coat pocket and pulled out a keyring. "Here," he said as he selected a key and dangled it in front of Princess. "Be a good girl and let us in."

She stared at the keyring. "Why me?"

"Because you're forty-five years younger, about two hundred and fifty pounds lighter, reasonably intelligent, and extremely cute. And because I told you to."

"God, I hate you." But she took the keys and climbed out.

Once she'd opened the gate, T-Rex drove through. Passing the telescope, he pulled around behind the adjacent control building. From here, the Jeep couldn't be seen from the road. He zipped up his parka and pulled on his hunter's cap, then opened the door and heaved himself out from behind the wheel. By then Princess had jogged over to meet him. Despite the cold, she seemed to be happy to be getting out of the car. Perhaps it was just the long ride up from Mass, but he thought it was probably the show tunes.

"Go back and shut the gate," he said as she handed over the keys. "No need to lock it. I just want to make sure that, if someone happens to drive by, they won't think anyone's here."

She nodded and trotted back to the gate while he trudged through the fresh snow, glad that he'd had the foresight to wear winter boots for this trip. The snow was falling harder now, beginning to form drifts against the control building's windowless concrete walls; they'd have to hurry if they didn't want to get stuck here.

T-Rex unfastened the door's dead bolt, then entered the six-digit security code into the all-weather keypad. A soft click from within, and he turned the knob and pushed the door open. A fluorescent ceiling fixture flickered to life, exposing a narrow hallway whose plaster walls were covered with astronomical photos and a vintage *E.T.* movie poster. It was nearly as cold inside the building as it was outside, but that was just as well; the computers, dish control systems, and other electronic instruments in here preferred cool temperatures.

Pulling off his gloves and kicking the snow from his boots, T-Rex fondly looked around the place. He'd spent countless hours here over the years, enough to almost consider it a second home. When he'd negotiated the terms of his resignation from UNE, one of the things he'd managed to retain was access to the radio telescope. The university had allowed him to keep that because they knew how important MARVIN was; most students weren't even aware that UNE owned a radio telescope, but the administration considered it an asset. So getting in was never a problem. The trick was making sure no one ever learned that he and Princess had been here at this particular day and time.

The door opened again and Princess came in, blond hair windblown and frosted with snow. T-Rex patiently gave her a minute to remove her mittens and stamp the chill out of her feet, then he led her down the hall to a door at the end. The room was dark when they came in, but not lightless; it glowed with dozens of diodes and LCD readouts. He flicked on the lights, and was rewarded by a soft gasp of amazement from the young woman beside him.

"Wow." Princess gazed in amazement about the small room. "This is just—"

"Awesome?"

She stared at him. "How did you know I was going to say that?"

"Just a hunch."

The walls of the small, windowless room were lined with computer mainframes, boxy gray units without manufacturer nameplates that stood side by side and in the center of the floor, packed into every available inch of space. They hummed softly from the high-voltage electrical system that powered the adjacent telescope. The computers operating the telescope itself had been built by NASA technicians a generation ago and had been periodically upgraded ever since. The newest computer, the big multi-spectrum frequency analyzer that endlessly shuffled through the natural radio signals collected by the dish in search of repeating patterns, was a more recent addition, hand-built by UNE electrical engineering students over the course of two years. The wiring was mainly below the floor and above the drop-ceiling panels, so it wasn't obvious that the computers comprised a digital network almost as complex as the human nervous system.

If the radio telescope could be thought of as an immense ear, then the control room was the brain that interpreted what the ear heard. And now, T-Rex quietly mused, he and Princess were about to play a trick on this giant ear and others just like it.

At the far end of the room was a bench; two IBM workstations stood on the bench, luminescent Mandelbrot patterns endlessly convoluting on their flatscreens. T-Rex checked the row of seven analog clocks on the wall above them. Each marked the local time at MARVIN's global radio observatory network. The area of the sky presently being scanned was depicted on an IBM computer on the desk, while another one beside it displayed the natural-source radio emissions MARVIN was picking up.

Just then, it was the Romanian dish's turn to search the sky. In another hour or so, the one in the Scottish highlands not far from Balmoral Castle would take over. When that two-hour sweep was done, the computer network guiding the search would hand off to the Vermont dish and another two-hour scan of an adjacent stellar region would commence.

"Have a seat, my dear." From beneath the bench, T-Rex pulled out a swivel chair that had always been just a little small for him. "Time to make history."

"Aweso—I mean, okay." Princess lowered herself into the chair. Without a word, she held out her hand. T-Rex reached into his coat pocket and pulled out a thumb drive no different from the one she'd used four months ago. Princess located a serial port on the back of the left-hand computer and plugged in the thumb drive; a tiny icon appeared on the screen, signaling that the external drive was engaged.

"Ready," she said.

T-Rex took a deep breath. For just a moment, he questioned whether this was something he really ought to be doing, and asked himself if it wasn't too late to stop now. Then the moment passed, and with it disappeared any doubts or hesitation he may have still had.

"All right, then," he said. "First, enter the declination and right-ascension for the cube's current position..."

Twenty-eight minutes later, they were done. As Princess pushed back her chair, T-Rex leaned over the bench and typed in a new set of commands to the keyboard. With a few short keystrokes, all digital records of their visit were deleted. Even if someone checked the system logbook, they would find nothing to indicate that anyone had been here since the last time Robbie Dollens was here.

"Come, my dear," he said quietly, gallantly holding her chair for her. "The time has come for us to make like phantoms and vanish."

With that, T-Rex ushered her out of the control room. A final pause to carefully make sure that everything was just as they'd found it, then he shut off the lights and closed the door. The snow they'd tramped in was already evaporating, and the hallway lights would go off as soon as he shut the door and locked it. The only evidence that they'd been there were their footprints and tire tracks, and the snow would fill them before the night was over.

The Jeep started without any problem. They drove out through the gate, where T-Rex paused to let Princess get out to close and lock it behind them. As she did, he heard a loud, mechanical groan.

Twisting about in his seat, he watched through the back window as, with slow and stately movements, the dish rotated and tilted in another skyward direction. It was about to perform the task that he and Princess had secretly given it.

He smiled. It wouldn't be long now. Just enough time, in fact, for them to get home.

First Contact

In the silent darkness of his study, Dr. Theodore Reggs sat at his desk. Fingers steepled together, face backlit by his computer screen, he contemplated his crime as he waited for it to unfold.

The computer displayed two images. The larger of the two was a seemingly endless scroll of numbers coming to him from MARVIN: a star's catalog name, along with its declination and right ascension, and finally—after a minute or so—the word *NEG*, meaning that the network radio telescope that had just scanned that particular star for signs of intelligent life had come up with a negative result.

As T-Rex watched, the radio observatory in Scotland rejected another star and immediately began examining its closest neighbor in the sky. That part of MARVIN's nightly sweep, though, would soon be over. In just a few minutes, the Scottish telescope would automatically hand off the search to its partner in Vermont, and with barely a pause the Wilner Radio Observatory would continue the long, quiet quest for extraterrestrial life in the universe.

The other image on the screen, the smaller one, was a window T-Rex had opened on the upper left side of the display. It depicted a couple of concentric circles, one within the other, with a small yellow dot at the center. An off-center arc overlapped and connected the two circles. The circles represented the respective orbits of Earth and Mars; the arc represented the trajectory and estimated position of MarsCube 4, apparently lost in space, its actual location known to only two people in the world.

Something softly rustled from across the room. T-Rex looked over at the couch. Princess was curled upon it, wool blanket wrapped around her slender body, face half-buried in a throw pillow. She was tired from the long, cold road trip, but she'd turned down his offer to drop her off at the school and instead asked if she could spend the night at his place. He smiled. A thousand boys probably longed for her to say that to them. This wasn't the first time she'd slept on his couch, but tonight was special, and he didn't have to ask why she'd wanted to stay the night. She wanted to be here when MarsCube 4 called in.

Looking back at the screen, T-Rex checked the chronometer above the toolbar. 2157 EST, or 0157 GMT. In just three minutes, Scotland would hand off to Vermont. And a few minutes after that...

T-Rex peered through the darkened study at the bookcase where the small plastic model of MarsCube 4 stood. It wasn't hard to imagine the tiny spacecraft now, a little silver box with black rectangular wings and a dish antenna not much larger than the old satellite-TV receiver perched on the corner of his roof, sliding through the void. Perhaps it was deaf to all the entreaties sent to it from its controllers in Pasadena, but it wasn't mute... not for very much longer, at least.

Soon, MARVIN would hear from the errant MarsCube.

When he and Princess had used the radio telescope to make contact with MarsCube 4, they'd done so by transmitting on a UHF channel different than the ones used by NASA's Deep Space Network to communicate with their planetary probes. Furthermore, the new program Princess had sent three months earlier had instructed MarsCube 4 to respond only to messages containing a coded header known solely to herself and the professor. So the signal they'd sent earlier that evening could only be heard by the probe, and contained information that only MarsCube 4 could interpret; none of the five other MarsCubes in the vicinity would receive or respond to the signal.

The probe's SDR communications system received messages just on the UHF band, but it was capable of transmitting on the X band, the frequency range in which SETI scientists had traditionally searched for extraterrestrial radio signals such as Benford beacons. In about ten minutes, MarsCube 4 would do just that. A series of carefully-timed pulses, beginning with a single one, followed quickly by three more, then five, then seven, then eleven, and so on through the first ten prime numbers, would be sent, followed by a much longer pattern of pulses that were unintelligible and yet couldn't possibly be coming from a natural radio source such as a neutron star or a burster.

The pattern would reach its end and would be followed by exactly ten seconds of silence. Then the sequence would repeat, beginning with the first prime number. A textbook example of what SETI scientists expected to hear from an extraterrestrial civilization attempting to make contact with another race somewhere in the galaxy.

After five repetitions, the prime number sequence would be followed by a two-minute burst of pulses that would follow another sequence that would be unquestionably artificial and yet absolutely and utterly meaningless. Like what you'd get from a chimpanzee randomly tapping away at a telegraph key: there's undoubtedly a mind behind the output, but that mind can't be understood because the message is content-free.

T-Rex laughed quietly at the thought of legions of astronomers, mathematicians, linguists, exobiologists, and psychologists who'd soon be pulling their hair out trying to decipher the indecipherable. A little bit of revenge there against his colleagues in the SETI community who'd cast him out.

Since the UNE radio telescope would be online at the time, the Vermont dish would be the first one in the MARVIN network to receive the bogus signal. But once it did, and the multispectrum frequency analyzer in Vermont determined that the sequence fit within the parameters for artificiality established by T-Rex and the other MARVIN scientists, it would immediately red-flag the findings and send an urgent email to everyone directly involved with the project... beginning with Dr. Theodore Reggs, professor emeritus of the University of New England, who'd receive the news before everyone else.

The dish in northern California would be unpinned and realigned to locate and track the radio source once it came above the horizon. The MARVIN radio telescopes west of it would do the same once Earth's rotation brought the mysterious object into their range as well. By then, T-Rex figured that all his colleagues would be wide awake, no matter where in the world they lived. They'd be staring at their screens, scrawling red circles about numbers on fanfold sheets of printout, dancing around the room, scaring spouses, kids and pets, feverishly sending emails to one another, shouting over the phone, opening bottles of champagne or whiskey or beer or whatever else was handy, and otherwise going apeshit.

And all the while, the signal pattern would repeat, over and over again, slowly but gradually moving down the X-band in a way that would mimic something few people expected to find from an extraterrestrial signal: a doppler shift.

And that would only be the beginning...

With no fuss whatsoever, the header at the top of the screen changed slightly, signaling anyone who might happen to be watching that Scotland had just handed off to Vermont. It wouldn't be long now.

"Di?" T-Rex called softly. "Sweetie, are you awake?"

The girl rolled over on the couch and continued to snore just under her breath. The professor crumpled up a wad of scrap paper and hurled it at her, catching her on the back of her head. "Princess Diana?" he called more loudly. "Wake up, your highness!"

"Heywuzzafugd'ya…" Princess pried open her eyes and rolled over again. "Izzitime?"

"Uh-huh. Get up, your majesty. Let's go make history."

Yawning in a most unladylike manner, Princess lurched to her feet. Clutching the blanket around her shoulders, she came over to the desk. For a minute or so, the two of them watched in silence as the row of stellar coordinates scrolled down the screen, each one with a NEG beside it. Then it came to one in particular and stopped.

There was a long, long pause. And then the word POS appeared beside it. Five seconds passed, and then the phone beside the computer rang.

"Okay," T-Rex said as he reached over to take the robot call from Vermont, "you're on."

Princess nodded. Yawning, she shuffled into the dining room where she'd set up her laptop computer. Time to tip off the media.

TKA-01

The street outside the university auditorium was lined with TV news vans parked bumper to bumper along the sidewalk. Looking down from an upstairs office window, T-Rex reflected that their satellite dishes resembled miniature versions of radio telescopes. Campus police stood in the street, directing traffic to a nearby visitors lot. Just below the window, a tent had been set up as a media center; a little while ago, reporters, producers, and cameramen were standing in line to receive their lanyards and press kits. A couple of faces seemed familiar; at least one belonged to a network anchor.

The last time he was on campus, there had been demonstrations demanding his removal. There was still one sole holdout, a hairy undergraduate who'd shown up wearing a Chewbacca onesie and carrying a cardboard sign reading *T-Rex Is A Racist*. But the reporters had no idea what this was all about, and even if they did, they probably wouldn't have cared. In any case, campus police had ordered the kid to stay on the other side of the street. As T-Rex watched, the kid—cold, lonesome, and ignored—gave up. He dropped his sign on the sidewalk and skulked away.

T-Rex smiled. "G'wan home," he murmured. "Your mommy's calling."

"Ted?"

Hearing his name, he turned to find Jodi McCabe behind him. "Ready?" she asked. "It's time to go."

"Sure. You bet." T-Rex gave her a nod that she returned with a nervous smile. Like her, he'd worn his best clothes today. For him, this was a tweed jacket he'd bought at Macy's five years ago and a tie he hadn't put on in nearly twice that long. As he stepped away from the window, Jodi took his hand and gave it a reassuring squeeze.

"You'll do fine," she said softly. "This is your big moment, you old dinosaur... I'm glad it's come for you."

He was about to reply when David Rycroft came up to them. "I'll open with a few remarks, then hand it over to you, Dr. McCabe, so you can introduce Dr. Reggs—"

"If it's all the same," Jodi said, "I'd just as soon not. No offense, David, but I don't think it's necessary. Everyone here knows who Ted is."

"Very well." Rycroft wasn't ready to step aside quite yet. "Just one more thing. Dr. Reggs... or may I call you Ted?"

T-Rex remembered the last time Rycroft asked him this, even if he didn't. "Dr. Reggs will be fine."

Rycroft frowned; no, he wasn't getting off the hook that easy. "Dr. Reggs, I hope that, when you're addressing the news media today, you'll forget the unpleasantness of last fall. Again, I'm sorry for the circumstances that forced your resignation, but I hope that you'll remember that the school let you continue your research as a professor emeritus, and if it weren't for our generosity—"

"I shall keep this in mind." He looked at Jodi again. "If you will...?"

Stifling a smile, Jodi grasped his arm and led him from the office. University cops had positioned themselves outside; they held back the reporters in the hall who'd been trying to talk their way in for an interview. These were the clueless ones; the smart guys had already ferreted out T-Rex's email address and had been flooding him with offers to talk for cash. He'd decided to let them sweat for a little while until he picked the two or three best offers. A little pocket change until he landed a fat six-figure book deal. This wasn't the purpose for what he was doing, but there wasn't any point in passing up a chance to make a few bucks.

And, as Princess said, it didn't suck to be famous.

The auditorium was standing room only, although he could barely see anything beyond the glare of camera lights in front of the stage. The press had taken nearly every available floor seat, with others parked along the walls, while up in the balcony were the handful of students and faculty members lucky enough to get in. Although he couldn't see her up there, T-Rex had made sure that Princess got a seat.

On the other hand, he'd made no effort to do the same for Luis Tuleja. Jodi told him that he'd tried to claim a spot on stage, but she'd denied him a chance to attach himself to something in which he'd played no role. T-Rex wasn't surprised by Luis's opportunism; what was amazing was how shamelessly he went about it.

Camera shutters began clicking the moment he and the others walked on stage. Like a swarm of cicadas, they became a constant aural background even after he and Jodi took their seats and Rycroft stepped up to the podium. The university president took a moment to welcome the members of the press to the campus on such an historic occasion, and then went about introducing "our esteemed colleague and recently retired professor emeritus."

As T-Rex expected, no mention was made of the reasons for his abrupt retirement several months earlier. Rycroft spoke only of his "outstanding record as a research astrophysicist" while describing him as "a leader in the ongoing search for extraterrestrial intelligence," a quest that, "after generations of effort, has finally yielded a definite answer to the question, 'Are we alone in the universe?'" And with that rhetorical flourish, the president yielded the podium to Dr. Theodore Reggs.

T-Rex had to wait nearly a minute for the applause to subside before he was able to speak. When he did, he began with a formal repetition of what the press already knew, thanks to the info that Princess had artfully leaked to *Hot Science*. When she'd told him which web site she'd picked to anonymously forward the draft report he'd written for the other MARVIN scientists, he'd been horrified. The creation of a former *New York Post* editor and catering to geeks, faddists, and science fiction movie fans, *Hot Science* was known for pieces like "The Ten Sexiest Women in Marine Biology" and "Killer Robots: Are They Right For You?" Hardly a respected news source; he would have preferred the *New York Times* or the *Washington Post*.

"It gets almost a million hits a day," Princess countered. "Do you want respectability, or do you want to get the news out fast?"

She was right. Within twelve hours of *Hot Science* reporting an anonymous email sent by someone presumed to be associated with Project MARVIN—T-Rex, of course, firmly denied that it'd been him—the initial blog post had gone viral. And in three days, word had spread around the world: first the Internet news media, then to major TV networks, and finally the establishment press.

Protocols established by the International Academy of Astronautics called for consultation with the heads of the United Nations before any official announcement of contact with an alien race was made. But that didn't fit into T-Rex's plans; hence the anonymous email message sent to the social media source most likely to scream it to the world without restraint or verification. Hence, the U.N. Secretary-General got the news of first contact the same way everyone else did, from Facebook.

And so, just four days after his surreptitious visit to Moose Creek, T-Rex found himself facing a battery of lights, lenses, and microphones. He couldn't help but grin, but not for the reasons everyone assumed, for in that moment he experienced a sense of surreal detachment. A few months ago, he'd been forced to resign in disgrace. And now...

You idiots! he wanted to shout. *You fools! You fell for one scam and now you're falling for another!*

But he didn't.

Instead, T-Rex cleared his throat. "Gentlemen and ladies," he said, his voice calm and even, "humanity has received its first confirmed signal from an extraterrestrial race... and they're closer than we ever expected they'd be."

For the next twenty minutes or so, T-Rex patiently led an impatient news media through a tour of Project MARVIN, explaining its facilities, research methodology, and objectives. On Jodi's advice, he used accessible, non-technical terms, avoiding jargon whenever possible; for details, he referred his audience to the copies of the formal letter to

The Doppler Effect and Other Stories

Astrophysical Review included in their press packets. In short, the story went like this:

Four nights earlier, at exactly 2237 hours EST, the Project MARVIN radio telescope operated by the University of New England in Moose Creek Valley, Vermont, sent an automatic phone alert to his home in Springfield. An identical call was also made to the observatory's on-site operator, but since he was in Florida on vacation, Dr. Theodore Reggs was the first to respond; therefore, he was credited as the official discoverer.

The signal picked up by MARVIN was transmitted at a base frequency of 10.6 gigahertz on the X band, slightly higher than the frequencies used by American, Russian, Indian, and Chinese spacecraft. It consisted of a short string of prime numbers, followed by a long series of binary numbers that, while forming no message that could be easily interpreted or deciphered, was inarguably not the product of any natural phenomena, but rather intelligent in origin. When the sequence began to repeat, Dr. Reggs immediately sent email to the other observatories in the MARVIN network, urgently requesting verification of the signal's existence and assistance in determining a possible point of origin.

Confirmation was quick in coming. The MARVIN dish in northern California detected the signal a little more than an hour later when it rose above the eastern horizon. But while the direction appeared at first glance to be somewhere in the Fornax constellation, parallax measurements soon established a much closer point of origin.

T-Rex paused. Silently counting to ten, he let the drama sink in before revealing the one thing that hadn't been leaked to the press.

"We're calling the signal TKA-01," he said, "with TKA standing for 'Transient Kuiper Anomaly.' We've tentatively traced its point of origin to a source within the outer reaches of our solar system. That is, it is an as-yet unseen object in the Kuiper Belt, approximately nineteen and a half billion miles from Earth."

The Calculations of a Lie

T-Rex is interrupted by a knock at the door. While he'd been speaking, Princess left to go down the hall to the vending machines. Dandridge gets up and opens the door for her; she comes in with three cans of soda clasped between her hands. She gives the Diet Dr. Pepper to T-Tex, the Coke to Dandridge, and keeps the Orange Crush for herself, then settles back into her place on the bed.

"Thank you, my dear." T-Rex cracks opens his soda and takes a sip. "As I was saying... if it wasn't enough that I'd announced MARVIN discovering a signal from space, then the revelation that it was coming from our own backyard drove everyone right up the wall." He grimaces. "I anticipated that there would be some sort of reaction, sure, but if I'd expected what was going to happen..."

"You think you carried the hoax too far?" Dandridge asks, and T-Rex reluctantly nods. "In what way? By claiming that the signal emanated from somewhere within the solar system?"

"Yes, but—" T-Rex raises a finger "—it was necessary to do so. I realized that, once the other MARVIN observatories attempted to figure out the location by calculating its distance via stellar parallax measurement, they'd notice that its proper motion was changing faster than an interstellar object should be."

"So that's why you claimed it was coming from somewhere relatively close to Earth," Dandridge asks, and T-Rex nods again. "Then how—?"

"Parallax observation for radio astronomy within the solar system isn't so precise that it can't be fooled. One of the reasons why I deliberately waited a few months after Princess shut down NASA's link with the MarsCube before sending the new program was to let it get sufficiently far from Earth for its signal to become difficult to trace. By then everyone had written off MarsCube 4 as lost for good, so they didn't suspect that it was the source. But I did all this one better by programming the SDR to incrementally change the transmitter frequency in a manner that created the illusion of the Doppler shift you'd expect to see from a distant radio source that's slowly coming closer."

"So the estimated distance the other observatories arrived at was—?"

"Two hundred and ten AU's from the Sun. They couldn't see it, of course, but that didn't surprise anyone. Unless your starship is as big as the *Death Star* and it's lit up like the *Enterprise*, there's no way you can image something like that."

"What about Hubble? Didn't NASA point it in that direction?"

"Oh, sure they did. One of the first things NASA tried to do was get the Space Telescope Science Institute at Johns Hopkins to aim Hubble in the direction of the transmissions. But Hubble is meant for studying large, bright objects at interstellar distances, not small dark objects within our own system. So when Hubble didn't find anything, that was the logical explanation."

T-Rex smiles. "If we'd done this a few years from now," he adds, "after the new James Webb Space Telescope goes up, things might have been different. Its resolution is a lot greater than Hubble, so failure to find something out there might have raised suspicions. But because Webb isn't yet in orbit and because I made sure that the source appeared to be coming from somewhere relatively close to us, no one tumbled to the gag."

A quiet laugh. "Besides, everyone wanted this thing to be real. That helped a lot. You can fool yourself if, deep down inside, you want to be fooled."

"Slick. Very slick." Then Dandridge thinks about it for a second and shakes his head. "Wait... no, I don't understand. If the idea was to fake an alien spaceship heading for Earth, wouldn't everyone realize that it was a hoax when it never got here?"

"No, because at a certain point, the frequency shifts would have started changing in the other direction, gradually moving back up the band. This would have given the impression of another doppler shift... the sort you'd expect to see if a craft was *leaving* the system again."

Dandridge stares at him. Suddenly, he gets it. "So," he says slowly, "the ship comes into the outer solar system, transmits a signal toward Earth—"

"A signal that's unquestionably artificial in nature, but ultimately indecipherable because there's no meaning behind the pattern."

"—and then turns about and leaves again, before anyone can discover that it's not real." Dandridge finds himself admiring the man seated on the other side of the room. "And the point was... what? Credit for being the scientist who discovered the first evidence of intelligent life in the universe? Or was it just revenge?"

T-Rex shakes his head. "If you think I'd get any satisfaction from taking credit from a scientific hoax, then you misunderstand who I am. I admit that it was sweet to hijack Luis's MarsCube, but revenge wasn't the point, either."

"And that is...?"

"I hate to say it: the point got lost when the plan backfired."

"What he's trying to say," Princess says quietly, "is the shit hit the fan."

Socialist Gay Death Armada from Planet X

"*I have no doubt whatsoever,*" said the man on T-Rex's living room TV, "*that Earth is facing an imminent invasion from space.*"

Large and burly, wearing old-style horn-rim glasses and an Abe Lincoln beard, he fixed his unblinking gaze upon the Fox News reporter. The newswoman—did Fox have any females on the air who weren't blondes?—didn't seem to be the slightest bit incredulous. Leaning forward in her studio chair, she listened to him as if he was the very font of scientific wisdom.

"*And it's your contention that TKA-01 represents the vanguard of an alien race that intends to attack us?*" she asked.

The alleged "world famous astronomer and alien expert"—universally regarded in the SETI field as a crank—shook his head. "*No, not the vanguard, but the armada itself. Very reliable sources have told me that the source behind TKA-01 has already been discovered and analyzed by the government's top scientific experts, and they've determined that an entire fleet of alien vessels is lurking within the Kuiper Belt. In fact, since its position is close to the orbit of the hypothetical tenth planet of our solar system—*"

"*The ninth planet, you mean.*"

A cynical smile. "*Yes, well, that's what the liberal scientific establishment would have you believe.*" The smile vanished. "*But Pluto is indeed the ninth planet, and so it's entirely possible... practically a fact, really... that the signals have originated from Planet X, which aliens are using as a base of operations for the upcoming—*"

T-Rex screamed and hurled the remote at the TV. It didn't break the plasma screen, but instead broke apart as if it was a cheap toy, scattering batteries across the floor. Princess flinched. Sitting beside him on the couch, she slid a couple of inches away, putting distance between herself and the professor.

"Sorry." He shook his head. "There's only one thing I hate more than football, and that's stupidity."

"That's okay," she said meekly. "Who was that guy?" One positive thing had been achieved by the demolition of the remote, at least; the channel was changed, and now they were watching *SpongeBob*. "He said he was a scientist, but I didn't hear him say where he—"

"The charlatans always claim they're scientists," T-Rex growled. "Yeah, I know that clown. He was at NASA a long time ago, a mission planner at Marshall Space Flight Center. Then he went around telling everyone they've got a flying saucer inside a shuttle hangar at Cape Canaveral, and they jettisoned him. Now he makes his living on cable news shows as the go-to guy for UFO stories." He made a rude noise with his lips. "I don't know if he's really a screwball or just a bottom-feeder. Either way, he's only the latest, if not the loudest."

"Is it really that bad?" Climbing down from the couch, Princess crawled across the floor, collecting the bits and pieces of the remote. Hearing a disgusted snort from him, she glanced over her shoulder at T-Rex. "Hey, I'm a student, remember? I don't have time to watch TV all day."

"Glad to hear it," T-Rex said drily. "It means you won't grow up to work for Fox News." She glared at him. "My apologies... didn't mean it." He sighed and rubbed his eyes. "At least you didn't get yourself publicly involved with this. If you knew what I've been dealing with—"

"I know a little." Sitting cross-legged on the floor, Princess started putting the remote back together again. Behind her, SpongeBob was singing a happy song; she clicked off the TV the moment she had the remote reassembled. "The whole thing's gone crazy, hasn't it?"

T-Rex didn't answer that. He gazed at the blank screen, watching a reality show that existed only in his mind's eye. If he were to give his imaginary program a name, though, it would have to be *Who's The Biggest Asshole?*

And he'd be the star.

At first, the reaction to his announcement had been what he'd anticipated. Excitement. Astonishment. A certain amount of alarm, yes, even uncertainty, but nonetheless tempered by a sense of wonder, the revelation that the human race was not alone in the universe. Princess's favorite exclamation was what he'd expected, and that was what he'd received: this was, indeed, awesome.

And then, fear began to set in.

He didn't know how or where it started, but when it did, it happened fast. Somewhere in the vast, media-fed clot of facts, news, opinion, distortion, misinformation, and outright lies, a voice asked, *What if TKA-01 is hostile?*

The voices became more numerous, more anxious. What if the ship isn't here for peaceful reasons? What if the message isn't a mere greeting, but a demand to surrender? What if the aliens aren't like Spock or E.T. but more like the ones in *V*? Or *Alien*? Or *Independence Day*? What if there's not just one ship, but many? What if... what if... what if...?

Of course, no one could give assured answers. The message was beyond interpretation because it had no content; the source was indeterminate because it was little more than an electronic echo. Like a magician's stage trick, it was all a clever illusion, only formed by computer code and microwaves rather than smoke and mirrors.

But this trick had gone wrong.

When he and Princess had written the program for MarsCube 4's SDR, they'd intended the signal to gradually increase until it hit 12.0 gigahertz, then began to decline at the same rate before suddenly ceasing entirely. This would have created the illusion that the approaching spacecraft had briefly entered the outer reaches of the solar system, then turned around and left before crossing Neptune's orbit. With any luck, this would have occurred before someone figured out that the Doppler shifts couldn't possibly be occurring at the distance everyone believed they were, and began looking for another explanation.

And then the program failed.

Perhaps they'd written it incorrectly. Maybe the SDR had misinterpreted their instructions. Whatever the reason, though, the fadeout didn't happen when it was supposed to. Instead, the frequencies continued to travel up the band, the signal pattern repeating itself faster and faster, increasing at a minute yet exponential rate, suggesting that the ship was inexorably coming closer...

And not turning around and leaving, as it was supposed to.

Naturally, all attempts to contact the "alien starship" were being ignored. Princess had instructed the space probe to disregard all messages except the one from Vermont she and the professor had sent, and now the silence was becoming distinctly ominous.

And meanwhile, the ship was apparently coming closer, and closer, and closer.

As linguists struggled to the translate the untranslatable, and the talking heads blathered, and the blogosphere became filled with cranks, kooks, and paranoids of every persuasion, public pressure rose for someone somewhere to Do Something. The Westboro Baptist Church blamed gays; a handful of their members showed up at the Marshall Space Flight Center in Alabama, carrying signs proclaiming that God hates fags. And Rush Limbaugh contended that liberals, socialists, and Hillary Clinton must have *something* to do with it.

Since it had become obvious to everyone that the alien vessel was most likely hostile, politicians responded, as they always did, with quick and immediate speeches. On Capitol Hill, demands were made for NASA to pull the shuttle fleet out of the museums, restore them to flight status, then pack them with lasers and send them into orbit. And if that wasn't feasible, then the U.S. needed to retarget its nuclear arsenal for deep space and launch those babies as soon as we saw the whites of their six, eight, or ten eyes.

In a rare press conference, the president made a brief appearance in the White House press room to tell reporters that his administration would do everything it could to defeat "this huge, huge alien threat." As usual, details were not offered. He refused to answer any questions and left quickly, sniffling.

T-Rex was summoned to appear before the Senate Science Committee. He traveled to Washington feeling as if he was going to have a heart attack any moment, and practically dripped with sweat as he sat at the witness table along with three other SETI astronomers associated with MARVIN. But no one asked him the question he dreaded the most, whether it was possible the whole thing was nothing more than an elaborate hoax. That possibility had only been raised by a handful of cranks and conspiracy theorists, and no one took it seriously. Instead, the senators wanted to know whether he or the others had any clues as to the aliens' possible motivations, and when Dr. Reggs expressed his opinion that the visitors were probably benign and meant no harm at all, a Texas senator accused him and the other scientists of being dangerously naïve.

Since then, T-Rex had hidden in his house, refusing to pick up the phone and coming to the door only reluctantly. He avoided looking at his email; the stuff he was getting ranged from crazy to desperate to homicidal, and since he'd lost count of the number of death threats he'd received, he could only hope that none were serious. So he sat on the couch, surfed the cable channels, and wondered whether it was possible to drive his Jeep all the way to the Andes, the only place he might possibly find someone who'd never heard of TKA-01.

"How are people taking it at UNE? Other students, I mean?" He wasn't really interested; he was just trying to find something to talk about.

"The school set up a place on campus where we can go for counseling." Princess wasn't looking at him. "We were told that it was okay to go there and cry if we feel the need. And they've provided nap mats and Play-Dough, too."

"How appropriate. So glad to hear they're respecting your maturity."

Princess didn't reply. She gazed straight ahead, as if thinking intently. "Maybe if—" she began, then stopped herself.

"Go on. What were you going to suggest?"

"Maybe if we went back up to Vermont, we could send another signal to the MarsCube. Change the SDR so that it does what we meant to do... make it look like it's turning around and going away. Or even shut down the transmitter completely."

"You mean, make the ship disappear. *Poof...* problem solved." He sighed. "I thought of that already. Robbie is back home. He and his wife returned as soon as the news broke. There's no way we could go up there without them seeing us, and he'd want to know what we're doing when we start fooling around with the dish."

Princess shrugged. "So I'll just access the computers from here. We know the passwords."

"We can't do anything from here without him noticing on the control shack's computer, which he checks every day." T-Rex shook his head. "Nice thought, darling, but that's not an option." Again, he let out his breath. "I should have let the joke go on for a little while, then gone public and revealed what I'd done. Prove to the world that everything you read on the Internet isn't necessarily true. That was the point I originally wanted to make."

"I know." Princess got up from the floor, came over to sit down beside him. "But everything happened so fast, and people—"

"People panicked." He looked at her. "Do you remember what President Roosevelt said during the Great Depression, when the whole country was going nuts because the stock market crashed and the banks were failing?"

"Umm... yeah. 'The only thing we have to fear is fear itself.'"

"Exactly. Well, it's gotten to where everyone is now afraid of everything. I'm not just talking about TKA-01. It's—"

The phone rang. It was on a side table next to where Princess had been sitting. T-Rex could have easily reached over and picked it up, but instead he covered his face with his hands. "Get that, will you please?" he asked. "Whoever it is, tell 'em I'm not here and take a message."

Getting up from the floor, Princess hurried over to the phone and picked it up. "Hello?... yes, this is Dr. Reggs' residence... no, I'm sorry, he's not here just now. I'm his assistant. May I take a message?"

She was quiet for a minute or so, listening to whoever had called. As T-Rex watched, her mouth slowly fell open and her face became pale. For the first time since he'd met her, Princess Diana Kirby seemed to be really and truly frightened.

"Uh-huh... uh-huh... okay... sure, I'll let him know... I'll have him call you when he gets back... bye." Princess put down the phone, and for a moment she didn't say anything. Then she looked at him.

"We're busted," she whispered.

Nothing to Fear

"I always had a sneaky suspicion," T-Rex says, "that if anyone figured it out, it would probably be another radio astronomer, because they're the ones with the knowledge and tools. And that's exactly what happened."

As he speaks, Dandridge steals a glance at his watch. He's been here for almost two hours. But while it's getting late, he needs to hear the rest, so he resolves to be patient just a little while longer.

"How did it happen?" he asks. "Who caught you?"

"A different project... RadioAstron, fifteen dishes scattered around the globe and linked with Russia's Spektr-R orbital radio telescope, conducting what's called Very Long Baseline Interferometry. In this instance, they've coordinated themselves with atomic clocks so that, when they're all operating at the same time, they've got the resolution power of a dish more than sixty-two thousand miles in diameter."

"I think I've heard of that. Aren't they searching for the supermassive black hole at the galactic center?"

"That's correct. And because VLBI has such precise ranging resolution, RadioAstron necessarily overlapped with MARVIN. So while they weren't looking for little green men, their dishes were pointed in approximately the same direction, and that meant they picked up the X-band transmissions MarsCube 4 was sending back to Earth."

"And they weren't fooled?"

"Oh, no... the frequency-shift trick worked on them, too. If it hadn't, they would've blown me—"

"Us," Princess says quietly.

"—us out of the water at once. No, it took longer than that, and it was a practically an accident when it happened."

T-Rex pauses to take another sip from his Dr. Pepper. As he does, Dandridge checks his watch once more. When he looks up again, he sees that Princess has noticed him doing so. The wariness has returned to her eyes.

Has she figured him out? He quickly glances away, hoping she'd trust him just a little while longer.

"It was a grad student working at the Russian dish," T-Rex goes on. "Young lad probably not much older than Di here. He was going through the printouts of everything RadioAstron had picked up in the past six weeks or so, a routine procedure to earmark the junk the VLBI picks up, when he noticed something unusual... a UHF signal transmitted from Earth's surface to somewhere in space, occurring just hours before TKA-01 was detected. He considered this to be rather odd, so he compared his printouts with those of the RadioAstron dishes in the western hemisphere, and when he did that, he was able to pinpoint the source of the UHF signal."

"Our dish in Vermont," Princess says. "He found a record of the signal we sent to the MarsCube."

T-Rex nods. "The call I got a few nights ago was from one of RadioAstron's project directors. Once I managed to calm down a little, I called him back and we talked about what the kid in Russia had found. I told him I didn't know anything about any radio transmissions from Wilner, and suggested that there must be some sort of error, but even though he didn't come right out and say it, I knew that he knew I was lying. There were too many coincidences."

"They nailed us," Princess says. "And that's when we went on the lam."

Dandridge raises an eyebrow. "Why? You said this happened three days ago. If anyone really believed this was a hoax, you'd think they would have gone public with it by now."

"I know... and that confuses me, too. With so many people believing that an alien fleet is bearing down on Earth, I assume you'd want to let the public know that there's nothing to fear."

"Unless you *want* them to be scared." Princess is looking straight at Dandridge when she says it; this time, there's no mistaking her distrustfulness.

"No." T-Rex shakes his head. "I'm sorry, my dear, but we've discussed this many times, and you're letting yourself become paranoid." He gives her a fatherly pat on the ankle, then looks at Dandridge again. "Anyway, I packed up and fled the house as soon I got off the phone. The only person who knew where I was going was her, and she followed me the next day."

"We've been holed up here since then," Princess says. "He hasn't left the room since he checked in, and I've been bringing him all his meals. And I've been his go-between with you, too."

"That's when you emailed me?"

"That's correct," T-Rex says. "Eventually, the news is going to come out... as I said, I'm surprised it hasn't already... and so I determined that, when it did, it would probably be best if I'd already told my side before the blogosphere gets hold of it and distorts everything." He shrugs. "I've read a lot of your articles, so I picked you. She did the rest."

Dandridge lets out an exhausted sigh. This time he doesn't make an effort to hide looking at his watch. "Well, this is all very interesting, but it's getting late and—"

"Who's in the car?" Princess asks.

"What?" This startles him. "Excuse me?"

"I saw you when you came over from the diner. I was watching from the lobby. You parked away from the building, but when you opened the door to get out, the dome light came on and I saw someone in the back seat. Who is it?"

"There's no one else." Dandridge feels his face becoming warm. "I came alone."

"You must be mistaken." T-Rex casts her an admonishing glare. "Michael Dandridge is one of the most respected journalists around. He wouldn't—"

"Yeah, okay… okay." Princess's face turns red. She looks down at her lap, not meeting Dandridge's eyes. "Sorry," she mumbles. "Guess I'm wrong."

"Your eyes were playing tricks on you, that's all." It's a lame excuse, but it'll get him out of the room. Trying not to appear hasty, Dandridge puts away his notebook and pen, then picks up his recorder and switches it off. "Anyway, look… it's going to take me a couple of days to listen to the interview and look over my notes, but I'll get back to you before I reach out to any editors. The hoax may have been exposed by then, but I assure you that I won't say anything to anyone."

"Is that a promise?" Princess still isn't looking at him.

Dandridge ignores her. "In any case, I'll be in touch."

"Very well." T-Rex grunts softly as he gets up from his seat. Reaching across the bed, he holds out his hand. "Thank you for coming and spending so much time with us. I'll look forward to hearing from you soon."

Dandridge shakes hands with Dr. Reggs, then picks up his coat and leaves the room. He does his best to avoid Princess's gaze on the way out.

Leaving the motel through the lobby door, he begins to walk over to where he'd parked his car. Halfway there, he pauses to look back. The curtains of the second-floor room he judged to be T-Rex's are open; a slender figure is silhouetted against the light. Princess, watching him leave.

As soon as he's in the car, the man in the back seat asks, "What took so long?"

"You wanted me to interview him, didn't you?"

"Yeah, but it's freezing out here."

"Sorry." Dandridge puts the key in the ignition and turns on the engine so they can get some heat. "It took a while to get the whole story out of them. You said you wanted a complete confession—?"

"Did you get it on the record?"

For a second, Dandridge is tempted to not hand over the recorder. Until the moment that afternoon he'd arrived at David Rycroft's office for a scheduled interview with the UNE president, only to find a federal marshal and two FBI agents waiting for him, he'd been acting solely as a freelance journalist. But that ended when he'd learned that the email he'd exchanged with Princess had been intercepted—apparently the feds had discovered her connection to him when they searched T-Rex's house—and that these men wanted him to lead them to the fugitives and get a recorded confession. That's when he became an informant, albeit unwillingly.

If he'd had any balls, Dandridge tells himself, he would've chucked the recorder as soon as he left the room. But he doesn't want to go to prison, so he pulls it out of his coat pocket and passes it to the man sitting behind him.

"Thanks." The federal marshal touches the Replay switch, and they briefly hear T-Rex's voice—"*MARVIN was designed so that...*"—before he snaps the recorder off. "They're still in there, I take it," he asks as he puts it away."And both are unarmed?"

Dandridge snorts. "Who do you think they are, Bonnie and Clyde?"

"Just checking. Which room?"

"He's in 217. She's across the hall in 216." He hesitates. "What's going to happen to them?"

"Not my call. That's up to a judge and jury to decide. Okay, then..." The agent picks up a wireless transceiver from the seat beside him, holds it to his face. "Zulu, Alpha. Zulu, Alpha. Suspects in 217 and 216. Believed to be unarmed. Move in and apprehend. Over."

A moment passes, then a voice comes over the radio: "*Copy that, Alpha. Affirmative. Over.*"

About fifty yards away, the back door of the nearby moving van opens, disgorging four men in dark blue FBI windbreakers and ball caps. Two stride quickly toward the lobby doors while another two approach the side entrance. Peering at the second floor room he'd spotted earlier, Dandridge catches a glimpse of the drapes falling back in place.

Princess has spotted the feds. She and T-Rex know they're coming. He's too old and fat to run for it, but she has a slim chance at making a getaway if she abandons him. But Dandridge doubts she will. Whatever her other faults, Princess Diana Kirby is loyal to Dr. Theodore Reggs. He even wonders if she loves him, perhaps just a little bit.

The marshal opens the back door. "Your part is done, Mr. Dandridge. You're free to go. Your country appreciates the service you've done."

"Really?" Dandridge doesn't look at him. "I hope my country never finds out."

The marshal doesn't respond. The handcuffs clipped to the back of his belt jangle softly as he climbs out. Just before he shuts the door, though, he turns to Dandridge again. "You shouldn't be so hard on yourself. It's because of citizens like you that people have nothing to fear."

Dandridge watches as the marshal begins walking across the lot to join his team inside the motel. Then he turns on the headlights and drives away.

The author extends his appreciation to the following people for their advice and assistance in the research and development of this story: Dennis Wingo, President and CEO of Skycorp; Dr. Donald H. Edwards, Professor Emeritus of Neurophysiology, Georgia State University; Lauretta Nagel, Operations and Engineering Division, Space Telescope Science Institute; Ira Wilner, First-Class radio engineer; my friends Terry Kepner and Rob Caswell, and my wife Linda.

FROGHEADS

i

The shuttle fell through the clouds—clouds as dense as grey wool, separating purple sky and sun above from perpetual rain below—for what seemed like a very long time until the windows finally cleared and Venus's global ocean lay revealed: dark blue, storm-lashed, endless.

Engines along the spacecraft's boat-like underbelly fired, forming concentric circles of white-peaked wavelets that spread outward upon the ocean surface. Gradually the shuttle made its final descent until its hull settled upon the water. As careful as the pilots were, though, the splashdown was rough. A swift, violent jolt passed through the passenger compartment, shaking everyone in their seats, causing an overhead storage compartment to snap open and spill a couple of carry-on bags into the center aisle. Through the compartment, people cursed—mainly in Russian, although a few American obscenities were heard as well—and someone in the back noisily threw up, an involuntary act that was greeted by more foul language.

Ronson wasn't happy about the landing either. This wasn't the first time he'd traveled off-world, but landing on Mars was mild compared to this. He couldn't blame the guy a few rows back for getting sick. Although the shuttle was no longer airborne, nonetheless it remained in motion, slowly bobbing up and down as it was rocked by the ocean. He'd been warned to take Dramamine before boarding, and he was glad he'd heeded the advice.

Clutching the armrests, Ronson gazed through the oval porthole beside his seat. Rain spattered the outer pane, but he could still see where he was. Not that there was much to look at: ocean for as far as the eye could see—the Venusian horizon was about three miles away, nearly the same as Earth's at sea level—beneath a slate-colored sky blotted by clouds that had never parted and never would. The shuttle was supposed to make planetfall at Veneragrad, but the floating colony must be on the other side of the spacecraft. Unless, of course, the pilots had miscalculated the colony's current position and had come down—*landed* wasn't the proper word, was it?—in the wrong place.

That was a possibility. Ronson had spent the last four months in hibernation, but his waking hours aboard the *Tsiolkovsky* had shown him that Cosmoflot's reputation for ineptitude was well deserved. He'd just begun to consider the possibility that the shuttle was lost at sea when a tugboat came into view. Smoke belching from its funnel, the rust-flecked craft circled the shuttle until it passed out of sight once again. Several minutes went by, then there was a thump as its crew attached a towline to the shuttle's prow. The shuttle began to move forward again, the tug hauling it toward is final destination.

Everyone on his side of the passenger compartment peered through the windows as the shuttle pulled into Veneragrad, including the middle-aged Russian in the aisle seat who unapologetically leaned over Ronson as he craned his head for a look at the man-made island. Veneragrad was as utilitarian as only a Soviet-era artifact could be: a tiered hemisphere a kilometer in diameter, a shade darker than the ocean it floated upon, the long wooden piers jutting out from its sides giving it the appearance of an enormous, bloated water spider. Rickety-looking platforms, also constructed of native timber, rose as irregularly spaced towers from the outside balconies; they supported the open-top steel tanks which caught the rain and distilled it as the colony's drinking water. Radio masts and dish antennae jutted out at odd angles from near the top of the dome; a helicopter lifted off from a landing pad on its roof. An ugly, unwelcoming place.

"Looks bad, yes?" The man seated beside him stared past him. "Better than nothing... it's dry."

Ronson had already learned that his traveling companion spoke English, albeit not very well. His breath reeked of the vodka he swilled from a bag-wrapped bottle on the way down from orbit; he'd opened it as soon as the shuttle entered the atmosphere. "Is this where you live?" he asked, if only for the sake of being polite. "Is this your home, I mean?"

The other man barked sullen laughter. "This hellhole? No! My home, St. Petersburg. Come here to make money. Sell... um... ah—" he searched for the right word "—computers, yes? Computers for office."

Ronson nodded. He wasn't much interested in making friends with the businessman, but it appeared that conversation was unavoidable. "Whole colony, built in space above Earth, sent here by rockets," the businessman continued, telling Ronson something he already knew. "Dropped from orbit by para… para…"

"Parachutes."

"Parachutes, yes. Come down—" he lifted his hands "—*sploosh!* in water." He waved the bag toward the window. "People then build onto it. Wood from floating… um, forests, yes? Floating forests on moss islands."

"Yes, I see." Again, the businessman wasn't telling him anything new.

"Yes, you see." The Russian took another swig from his bottle, then offered it to Ronson. "So why you come here?"

Ronson shook his head at the bottle. There were several ways he could get out of this unwanted conversation. He opted for the easiest approach. "I'm a detective," he said, and when the businessman gave an uncomprehending look, he rephrased his answer in simpler, if inaccurate, terms. "A cop."

"A cop. Yes." The businessman gave him the distrustful look Ronson anticipated, then withdrew the bottle and settled back into his seat.

Ronson didn't hear from him again for the rest of the way into port. Which suited him well. He didn't want to talk about why he'd come to Venus.

ii

The heat hit him as soon as he stepped through the hatch. It was like walking into a sauna; the air was hot and thick, hard to breathe, humid beyond belief. The sun was larger and warmer here than on Earth, yet little more than a bright smear in the sky that heated up the atmosphere. Ronson began to sweat even before he reached the end of the wooden gangway that led to the hatch from the pier where the shuttle had been berthed. A fine, almost misty rain was falling, and it too was warm; he didn't know whether to take off the denim jacket he'd worn on the way down or keep it on. The dockworkers didn't seem to mind. Most of them wore only shorts, sneakers, and sometimes a rain hat, with the women wearing bikini tops or sports bras. They unloaded the bags from the cargo bay, and

Ronson took a few moments to find his suitcase before walking the rest of the way down the pier to the spaceport entrance.

There was only a couple of customs officers on duty, bored-looking Russians in short-sleeve uniform shirts who regarded the line of passengers with bureaucratic disdain. The officer Ronson approached silently examined his passport and declaration form, gave his face a quick glance, then put his stamp on everything and shrugged him toward an adjacent arch. No one had asked him to open his bag, but he knew what was about to happen. Sure enough, bells rang from the arch as soon as he walked through it. The weapon detector had found the gun he was carrying.

Just as well. It only meant that he'd meet the police sooner than he planned.

An hour of sitting alone in a detention area, another half-hour of angry interrogation by a port authority officer whose English wasn't much better than the businessman's, then Ronson was loaded onto an electric cart and spirited to police headquarters. Along the way, he got what amounted to a nickel tour of Veneragrad. The colony seemed to consist mainly of narrow corridors with low ceilings and low-wattage light fixtures, their grey steel walls decorated with grime, handprints, and stenciled Cyrillic signs, then the cart turned, passed through a broad doorway, and Ronson suddenly found himself in the city center: a vast atrium, its skylight ceiling a couple of hundred meters above the floor, with interior balconies overlooking a central plaza. As the cart cut across the plaza, Ronson caught glimpses of Veneragrad's daily life. Residents in shorts, vests, and T-shirts resting on park benches, hanging laundry on balcony clotheslines, standing in line in front of fast-food kiosks. A group of schoolchildren sitting cross-legged near a fountain, listening as their young teacher delivered a lesson. Two men in a heated argument; another couple of men watching with amusement.

A statue of V.I. Lenin stood in the center of the plaza. Incongruously dressed in a frock coat and high-collar shirt no Venusian colonist would be caught dead wearing—even inside the city, the air was tropically warm—he pointed toward some proud socialist future just ahead. But the statue was old and stained, and a broken string that might have once been a yo-yo dangled from the tip of his finger. The Communist Party was as dead on Venus as it was on Earth; it was just taking the locals a little longer to get rid of its relics.

The cart entered another dismal corridor, then came to a halt in front of a pair of battered doors painted with a fading red star. The port authority officer who'd questioned Ronson ushered him through the crowded police station to a private office, and it was here that he met Arkandy Bulgakov.

Veneragrad's police chief was about Ronson's own age, short and broad-chested, with the short-banged Caeser haircut that never seems to go out of style with European men. Seated at a desk piled with paperwork, he listened patiently while the officer delivered a stiff-toned report of the visitor's offense, punctuated by placing Ronson's Glock on the desk along with its extra clips. Bulgakov murmured something and waved the officer out of the room. He waited until the door was shut, then he sighed and shook his head.

"You're the same guy who emailed me a while ago about the missing kid?" His English was Russian-accented but otherwise perfect.

"That's me." Ronson motioned to an empty chair in front of the desk; Bulgakov nodded, and he sat down. "Sorry about the gun. I was going tell you about it when I reported in, but…"

"We don't allow private ownership of firearms. Didn't you know that?"

"I figured that my license might exempt me."

"No exemptions here. Only police are allowed to carry lethal weapons." Bulgakov's chair squeaked as he leaned forward to pick up the Glock; he briefly weighed it in his hand before opening a drawer and dropping it in. "I won't fine you, but you may not carry this. I'll give you a receipt. You may reclaim it when you leave."

"All right, but what am I supposed to use until then? I might need a sidearm, you know."

"To find a missing person? I doubt it." Catching Ronson's look, the chief shrugged. "You can buy a taser if it makes you feel better, but only if you're going outside the city. And if that's the case, then your chances of finding this fellow…"

"David Henry."

"…David Henry alive are practically zero. At any rate, he's not in Veneragrad, I can tell you that right now."

"That's what you told me five months ago," Ronson said, "and that's what I told my client, too. But the old man isn't satisfied. His kid was last seen here nearly a year ago, when he came to Venus on a trip his dad bought him as a college graduation gift."

Bulgakov raised a querulous eyebrow. "His father must be rich."

"The family has a few bucks, yeah, and the kid likes to travel. He's already been to the Moon and Mars, so I guess Venus was next on his list. Personally, if he was my boy, I would've given him a watch, but…"

"We don't have many tourists, but we do get some. His kind is not unfamiliar. Privileged children coming to see the wonders of Venus—" a brief smirk "—such as they are. They go out to the vine islands, take pictures, collect a few souvenirs. Now and then they get in trouble… a bar fight, dope, soliciting a prostitute… and they wind up here. But they eventually go home and that's the end of their adventure."

"That's not how it ended for him. He didn't come home."

"So it appears." Bulgakov turned to the antique computer on one side of his desk. He typed something into the keyboard, then swivelled the breadbox-size CRT around so that Ronson could see the screen. "This is him, yes?"

Displayed on the screen was a passport photo of a young man in his early twenties: moon-faced, arrogant blue eyes, sandy hair cut close on the sides and mousse-spiked on top. Good-looking but spoiled. The same boy in the picture his father had given Ronson when he'd visited the family home in Colorado Springs. "That's him."

Bulgakov turned the screen back around, typed in something else, paused to read the information that appeared. "He was registered at the GastinitsaVenera," he said after a few seconds, "but failed to check out. When my detectives went there to investigate, they were told that his luggage was found in his room, which apparently he hadn't visited for several days before his scheduled departure aboard the *Gagarin*. My men visited all the restaurants, shops, and bars, and although he'd been noticed in some of them, no one who worked in those places had seen him recently. And, of course, he failed to appear at the Cosmoflot departure gate to make his shuttle flight."

"You told me this already, remember? In your email." This was a waste of time. Which was what he'd expected; local police were seldom much help in missing person cases. Still, he always made a point of checking in with the cops. Professional courtesy, mainly, but there was always the chance that he might learn something he could use.

"So I did, and I imagine that you shared the information with *gospodin* Henry. And when he contacted the Russian consulate in Washington... he did this, yes?... he told them this as well." Bulgakov leaned back in his chair. "Very well, let me tell you what I didn't say in my email, because the government back home doesn't like to admit certain things and would be upset with me if I stated them in an official letter. On occasion... not often, but every once in a while... a young man like David Henry disappears while visiting Venus. Sometimes they wander down the docks after they've been drinking all night, fall off a pier and drown, and their bodies are devoured by scavenger eels. That has happened. Sometimes they go out on a boat tour with an unlicensed operator who's actually a criminal, who robs them, murders them, and leaves their bodies to rot on an island. That's happened, too. And sometimes... well, worse things."

"Such as?"

Bulgakov hesitated. "You've heard of *vityazka*, haven't you?"

"Yaz? Who hasn't?"

"That's the street name back home. *Vityazkaizkornia* is what it's called here." Bulgakov warmed to the subject. "It's derived from the same slickbark trees that grow on some of the vine islands that the pharmaceutical industry have bioharvested for *korenmedicant*, a clinical analgesic used in hospitals. But while *koren* comes from tree bark, *vityazka* comes from the roots. A narcotic as addictive as heroin..."

"And tastes just as bad when you smoke it," Ronson finished. "Know all about yaz. It's all over America and Europe."

Bulgakov scowled. He clearly didn't like being interrupted. "What you probably aren't aware of is exactly how the smugglers are getting it. Their growers... yaz croppers, we call them... go out to islands where slickbark trees are found. On the islands the drug companies have already harvested, they recover the tree roots left behind and process them for yaz. But everything that goes into this... cutting, boiling, curing... is hard work, not something anyone willingly wants to do. So sometimes they'll abduct some poor tourist who was in the wrong place at the wrong time and force them into hard labor."

"And you think that's what happened to David Henry? He was shanghaied?"

"I'd say that's a strong possibility."

Ronson slowly let out his breath. His job had just become much more difficult. "If you're right, then how do I find him? I understand those islands can drift quite a long distance…"

"There's thousands of them being carried by the ocean currents, and the croppers do a good job staying hidden. My people have always had trouble tracking them down. Locating the boy on one particular island will be difficult." Bulgakov paused. "However, there may be a way. As you Americans say, it's a long shot, but…"

"As we Americans say, I'm all ears."

"Talk to a froghead."

"A what?"

"Frogheads. The native aborigines. No one calls them Venusians… sounds like a bad movie. Anyway, they're intelligent—" another smirk "—although I wouldn't call them good company. And they see a lot of what goes on here."

"I can't even speak Russian. How am I supposed to talk to…?"

"I know someone who does. Mad Mikhail. You can find him down on the docks. Bring lots of rubles." Bulgakov smiled. "And chocolate, too."

"Chocolate?"

"You'll see."

iii

Mad Mikhail hung out on the waterfront. Everyone who worked there knew who he was; all Ronson had to do was follow their pointing fingers to a small shack set up on the dock where the tour boats were moored.

Mad Mikhail made sushi from whatever he'd been brought by local fishermen, which he then sold to tourists. When Ronson found him, he was sitting on a stool inside his open-sided shack, cutting up something that looked like a cross between a squid and a lion fish and wrapping the filets around wads of sticky rice. He was a squat old man with a pot belly and fleshy arms and legs, his dense white beard nearly reaching his collarbone. His skin was wrinkled and rain-bleached, and he wore nothing but a frayed straw hat and baggy shorts; when he looked up at Ronson, it was with eyes both sharp and vaguely mystical.

"Sushi?" he asked, his rasping voice thickened by a Ukranian accent. "Fresh today. Very good. Try some."

Bulgakov had warned Ronson not to eat anything Mad Mikhail offered him; whatever he failed to sell today, he'd simply keep until tomorrow, even if it had been spoiled by the heat and humidity. At least he spoke English. "No thanks. I've been told you can help me. I want to talk to a froghead."

Mikhail's eyes narrowed. "They are not frogheads. They are the Water Folk, the Masters of the World Ocean. You do not respect them, you do not talk to them."

"I'm sorry. I didn't know they—"

Mikhail slammed the long knife he'd been using down on the counter before him. "No one knows this! They call them frogheads, make jokes about them. Only I—" he jabbed a scarred thumb against his bare chest "—make friends with them when I came here over thirty years ago! Only Mikhail Kronow—!"

"You've been on Venus thirty years?" Ronson seized the chance to change the subject. "That means you would have belonged to one of the first expeditions."

"*Da.*" He nodded vigorously, not smiling but at least no longer shouting. "Second expedition, 1978. Chief petty officer, Soviet Space Force." A smile appeared within the white nest of whiskers. "The others went home, but I stayed. No one in Veneragrad been here longer...!"

"Then, Chief Petty Officer Kronow, you're the person I need to see." The best way to handle Mad Mikhail would be to appeal to his vanity. "I'd like to speak with the Water Folk... or rather, have you speak with them on my behalf, since you know them so well."

Mikhail's gaze became suspicious. "About what? If it's only a picture you want... *pfft!* Fifteen hundred rubles, they come up, you stand next to them, I take your picture. Take it home, put it on the wall. 'See, there's me with the frogheads.'" Disgusted, he spat over the side of the dock.

"I'm not a tourist, and I don't want a picture." Ronson reached into the pocket of his trousers—he'd have to buy shorts soon; his Earth clothes were beginning to stick to him—and produced the snapshot of David Henry his father had given him. Holding it beneath the shack's awning so that the rain wouldn't get it wet, he showed it to Mikhail. "I'm looking for this person. He came here almost a year ago, then disappeared. His family sent me here to find him."

Mad Mikhail took the photo, closely inspected it. "I do not know this boy," he said at last, "but the Water Folk would. If he went out to sea, they would have seen him. They see everyone who goes out into the World Ocean. You have chocolate?"

Ronson had purchased a handful of Cadbury bars at the hotel shop. He pulled them out and showed them to Mikhail. The old man said nothing, but simply gave him a questioning look. Ronson found his money clip, peeled off several high-denomination notes, held them up. Mikhail thought it over for a moment. "Very well," he said at last, easing himself down from his stool. "Come with me."

He emerged from the shack wielding a cricket bat, the sort an Englishman would carry to a sports field. Taking the money and the chocolate bars from Ronson, he led the detective down the dock, passing the boats tied up alongside. Captains and crewmembers lounging on their decks watched him with amusement; someone called to him in Russian and the others laughed, but Mad Mikhail only scowled and ignored them.

He and Ronson reached the end of the dock. A wooden light post rose above the water slurping against the dock's edge. The former cosmonaut raised the cricket bat and, with both hands, slammed it against the post: two times, pause, then two more times, another pause, then two more times after that. Mikhail stopped, peered out over the water, and waited a minute. Then he hit the post six more times, two beats apiece.

"This is how you summon fro… the Water Folk?" Ronson wondered if he was wasting his time.

"Yes." Mikhail turned his head back and forth, searching. "They hear vibrations, come to see why I call them. They do this for no one but me."

He'd barely completed his third repetition when, one at a time, three dark blue mounds breached from the rain-spattered surface just a couple of meters from the dock. With a chill, Ronson found himself being studied by three pairs of slitted eyes the color of tarnished pewter. Those eyes were all he could see for a few moments, then Mikhail held up the chocolate bars and the creatures swam closer.

"Move back and give them room," Mikhail said quietly. "Do not speak to them. They will not understand you."

One by one, the Venusian natives emerged from the water, climbing up onto the dock until they stood before Ronson and Mikhail. Each stood about a meter and a half in height, the size of a boy, and were bipedal, but their resemblance to humans ended there. They looked like a weird hybrid of a frog, a salamander, and a dolphin: sloping neckless heads, broad-mouthed and lipless, with protruding eyes; sleek hairless bodies, streamlined and mammalian, their slender arms and legs ending in webbed four-fingered hands and broad paddle-like feet; short dorsal fins running down their backs, away from blow-holes that vibrated slightly with each breath, that tapered off as reptilian tails which barely touched the wet planks of the dock.

Ronson couldn't see any anatomical differences between males and females, even though he knew that natives had two genders. Each were naked, their light blue underbellies revealing no obvious genitalia; only subtle splotches and stripes upon their wine-colored skin distinguished one individual from another.

And they smelled. As they came out of the water, his nose picked up a fetid, organic odor that reminded him of an algae bloom in summer. The stench was offensive enough to make him step back, and not just because Mad Mikhail had asked him to do so. If they came any closer, he was afraid he'd lose his lunch.

Ronson had recently read a magazine article about how an Egyptian-American scientist, who'd perished during a dust storm on Mars, had discovered just before his death certain genetic evidence linking *homo sapiens* to the native aborigines of the red planet. He wondered if much the same link might exist between the people of Earth and the Water Folk of Venus, and was both intrigued and disgusted by the thought he might be related, in some distant way, to these... frogheads.

Misha unwrapped the chocolate bars and offered them to the natives. As he did so, he addressed them in a low, warbling croak: *"Worworgwokkakrohwoka."* It sounded like nonsense to Ronson, but the Water Folk apparently understood him. The ones on the left and right bobbed their heads up and down and responded in kind—*"Worggakrohwohg"*—and moved toward him in a waddling, forward-hunched gait that might have been clumsy if it hadn't been so fast.

Only the native in the center remained where it was. It watched its companions with what seemed to be disdain as they each took a chocolate bar from Mikhail. When they opened their mouths, Ronson was startled to see that they contained rows of short, sharp teeth, with slightly longer incisors at the corners of the upper set. He was even more startled by the way they gobbled down the chocolate bars. Repulsively long tongues snatched the candy from their webbed hands; chocolate bars that even a hungry child might have taken a couple of minutes to eat were devoured in seconds. And yet the third froghead—Ronson couldn't help but to think of it that way—refused the bar that Mikhail held out to it.

"Why doesn't it take it?" Ronson whispered.

"I do not know," Mikhail murmured; he was a bit surprised himself. "They have never done that before." He raised his voice again. *"Waggakroh?"*

"Krohwogko!" The third froghead's tail swung back and forth in what seemed to be an angry gesture, its dull silver eyes narrowing menacingly. *"Krohwogkowakkawog!"*

"What did it say?"

Mikhail didn't respond at once. He held out the bar for another moment or two, then slipped it in his pocket. The other two Water Folk made hissing sounds that sounded like protests, but the third one stopped thrashing its tail and appeared to calm down a little. "The one in the middle is the leader," Mikhail said softly. "She…"

"You can tell it's a she?"

"Their leaders are always females. She refused the chocolate because… I think… she said it's poisonous." He shrugged. "I am not sure. I speak their language, yes, but some words of theirs I do not know well."

"But this is the first time you've seen any of them refuse chocolate?"

"Oh, yes. I've been giving it to them for many years. They love *kroh*. Nothing else like it on Venus. This is how I have made friends with them, learned how to talk to them." A thoughtful pause. "I do not know why one of them would refuse to take it. Very strange."

"Well, that's interesting, but I've got a job to do." Ronson pulled out David Henry's photo again. "Show this to them," he said as he handed it to Mikhail, "and ask if they've seen him."

The reaction was immediate. The moment Mikhail held up the photo, all three frogheads became agitated. Their tails swished back and forth, sometimes slapping the dock boards, as their heads bobbed up and down. They hissed, the leathery tips of their tongues slipping in and out of their mouths, and air whistled from their blowholes. Then the clan leader pointed to the photo and spoke in a rapid stream of angry-sounding croaks.

"Oh, yes… they recognize him, all right." Mikhail was just as surprised as Ronson. "And I do not think they like him very much."

"I kinda figured that. Ask if they know where he is."

Mikhail addressed the frogheads again, and once more they responded with head bobs and tail slaps. Then the leader bent almost double, shifted slightly to the left, and raised her tail to point to the left. Mikhail listened as she spoke to him at length, then he turned to Ronson.

"She knows where he is… on a moss island that's now some distance from here. She said she will lead us to him, but only if we will take him away."

"That's exactly what I want." Then he darted a look at Mikhail. "You said 'we'?"

Mad Mikhail smiled at him. "Unless you think you can speak to them, I will have to go with you, yes? And I will have to hire a boat, yes?"

Ronson knew without asking that the fee was going to be considerable. But he'd brought plenty of rubles with him, and he could always recoup his expenses from his client. "All right. Tell them that we…"

Mikhail didn't have a chance to translate. With no more conversation, the three frogheads suddenly turned and dove off the dock. Their bodies barely made a splash as they disappeared into the dark water. In an instant, they were gone.

"That was fast," Ronson muttered.

"We have an understanding. They will come back tomorrow morning." Mikhail turned away from the dock's edge, started walking back toward his shack. "Be here then. I will hire a boat and pilot to take us where they lead us. *Dasvidan'ye.*"

"See you later." At least he'd have time to buy new clothes and the equipment he'd need—namely a taser, seeing that was the only kind of weapon he was permitted to carry. Yet he couldn't help but notice the guarded expression on Mad Mikhail's face, and wonder if there was something the old man wasn't telling him.

iv

The *Aphrodite* was a beat-up fishing boat with rain-warped deck planks and a wooden hull that appeared to have been patched many times.

To Ronson's surprise, its captain was an American: Bart Angelo, middle-aged and a bit warped himself, smelling of fish and with ivory hair thinning at the top of his head. Forty thousand rubles was a lot to pay for the charter of a weathered old tub, but Ronson had little choice in the matter. He talked Angelo down to thirty-five thousand, and was grateful that he wouldn't have to also pay for a crew that the captain had decided to leave behind.

The frogheads returned, just as Mikhail said they would. Ronson assumed they were the same three he'd met yesterday, but he couldn't tell for sure. They didn't climb on the dock again, though, but instead lingered in the water beside the *Aphrodite*, half-submerged eyes steadily watching the men as they prepared to leave. Ronson wondered how they'd known which boat they'd use; Mikhail told them that they'd simply waited until they spotted him and Ronson again, then followed them to the *Aphrodite*.

"They are not animals," Mikhail added, giving him a stern look. "The Water Folk are intelligent... never forget that."

Hearing this, Angelo laughed out loud. "If they're so damn smart, then how come they keep getting tangled in my nets?"

"And what happens when they do?" Mikhail asked.

"They chew their way out." The captain finished counting the wad of money Ronson had just handed him and shoved it in his shorts pocket. "Goddamn critters cost me a repair bill whenever they do that."

Mikhail smiled knowingly. He didn't reply though, but instead went aft to loosen the stern line. Ronson heard him murmur something in Russian; he had no idea what he'd said, but it sounded rather amused.

The frogheads joined the *Aphrodite* as it chugged out of Veneragrad's harbor. They swam alongside until the boat passed the outer buoys, then moved out front and surfed its bow wake as the boat picked up speed, occasionally breaching the surface just as if they were dolphins. Ronson was concerned at first that the captain would run them down, but once Angelo throttled up the diesel engines to twenty knots, the Water Folk returned to their previous positions. They had no difficulty keeping up with the boat; never once did Ronson or Mikhail completely lose sight of them.

Veneragrad gradually disappeared behind them, becoming smaller and smaller until it faded into the misty, perpetual rain. Long before it vanished over the horizon, though, they saw other signs of the human presence on Venus. They passed fishing schooners and tour boats heading out for the day, and at one point crossed the wake of one of the massive sea dragon trawlers that prowled the global ocean for weeks on end. In the distance, they made out a tall structure erected on stilts: an oil derrick, probably owned by a Russian-Arab consortium, positioned just above a sea mount. Small single-mast sailboats took advantage of the mild weather and fair winds, but only a couple; Venus was not a planet for pleasure boating, and amateur sailors were the kind who often vanished and were never seen again.

By early afternoon, though, all other vessels had disappeared, and *Aphrodite* was the only boat on the ocean as far as the eye could see. Yet it wasn't alone. The first of the vine islands had come into view, and the Water Folk were leading the boat straight to them.

Ronson had never been a good student—he'd dropped out of college to join the NYPD, which in turn eventually led him to become a P.I.—but he remembered enough from his high school science classes to recall the planet's natural history. Billions of years ago, Venus had been Earth's twin sister, and even similar enough to Mars to make the panspermia hypothesis a possible explanation for a shared genetic heritage among humans, the Martian *shatan*, and frogheads. At some point in the planet's early eras, though, the Sun had raised the average global temperatures enough to cause a catastrophic greenhouse effect which melted the polar ice caps and formed the permanent cloud layer with its incessant rain. Eventually the entire planet was flooded, its lands masses inundated before tectonic shifts could keep them above the rising waters.

All that remained was a global ocean, yet beneath the watery surface were the old continents with their canyons and mountain ranges, like some vast Atlantis that would never again see the light of day. In some places, the ocean bottom lay only a dozen or so fathoms down, and it was here that underwater vegetation grew in abundance. One of the most common forms of marine plant life was a thick, ropey kind of seaweed that, once it grew large enough to become buoyant, tended to break free and float to the surface. Ocean currents gradually caused these weeds to clump together and form floating islands, some kilometers in length.

Over countless millennia, life evolved on these drifting isles. The frogheads were one kind; the slickbark trees that were a harvestable source of everything from timber to pharmaceutical drugs to yaz were another. And once humans learned how to travel between planets, the people of Earth discovered that Venus was a world rich with resources just waiting to be exploited.

Not everyone was happy about this.

"We are raping this planet." Mad Mikhail leaned against the starboard rail, watching the frogheads as they swam toward a vine island not much larger than a house. One of them had approached the boat and told Mikhail, in its croaking native tongue, that they needed a rest, so Angelo had grudgingly complied and dropped sea anchor near the next island they came upon. Now the Russian was in a reflective mood, breaking the pensive silence he'd maintained since leaving Veneragrad.

"Rape?" Angelo sat beneath the tarp strung as a canopy across the aft deck, eating a sandwich he'd made in the galley. "Don't talk about your sister that way... it's not nice."

Mikhail ignored him, as did Ronson. The captain had an ugly sense of humor; Ronson had discovered this when he'd joined him for a while in the wheelhouse, only to have Angelo start telling him jokes that grew progressively more disgusting until he found an excuse to leave. "How do you say that?" he asked, turning his back to the captain.

"We come here," Mikhail said, "and we take and we take and we take, but we give nothing back." He nodded toward the frogheads; they lay prone upon the island's matted weeds, vines, and moss, dozing in the midday heat. "They suffer the most. We steal their forests, pollute their water with oil, ruin their islands..."

"And then they hang around Veneragrad so they can mooch candy bars from you." Angelo shrugged. "Sounds like a fair trade to me."

"No. Not fair." Mikhail cast a cold glare at him. "Chocolate for a world... not a fair trade at all."

"Yeah, well... look who got 'em hooked on it in the first place." Noticing Ronson's quizzical look, Angelo sneered. "You mean you don't know? Chocolate is addictive to frogheads. Like cocaine, maybe even worse. Once they've had a taste, they gotta get more. And guess who got 'em started on it?"

"You lie!" Mikhail's face was red. "I was not the first to do this! One of my shipmates...!"

"Oh, sure. Maybe it wasn't you, but you're their number one pusher." Angelo tossed the remnant of his sandwich overboard, wiped his hands against his shorts. "And if you're not, then why don't you toss over those candy bars you brung?"

Mikhail looked away, avoiding the accusation Angelo had made. Ronson wondered if it was true. "One day, we will pay for what we have done here," he said quietly.

"Yeah, well… you're paying me for this trip and the day ain't getting any shorter." Angelo stood up from the barrel, headed for the wheelhouse. "Tell the froggies to rise and shine. I want to find this place and go home."

v

The captain didn't get his wish. At the end of the day, the frogheads still hadn't reached their destination, forcing *Aphrodite* to seek another island where it could anchor for the night. Again, the frogheads found a place to rest on its mossy, vine-covered banks.

As darkness fell on the ocean, Angelo opened a locker on the aft deck and pulled out a large net. Ronson thought at first that he intended to go trawling, but instead Angelo told him and Mikhail to rig the net above the boat, from the wheelhouse roof to poles erected at the stern, until the deck was completely covered. Angelo then switched off the deck lamps, and once the three of them went below he closed the curtains in the cabin portholes.

They'd barely finished dinner when Ronson discovered the reason why the captain had taken such precautions. From somewhere outside came the sound of wings flapping, punctuated by high-pitched shrieks. Mikhail explained that they belonged to one of Venus's few avian species: night shrikes, nocturnal raptors not much larger than the pelicans they vaguely resembled but dangerous nonetheless. The shrikes hunted in flocks, seeking prey near the islands where they nested; they had little fear of humans, and had been known to gang up on unwary sailors who ventured out on deck after dark. The nets would keep them away, and if that didn't work, a taser shot was sufficient to drive them off. Still, the best defense was to remain inside until daybreak.

Through the night, long after the three of them had crawled into their bunks, Ronson heard the shrikes prowling around the boat. Distant thunder and lightning flashes glimpsed around the edges of the porthole curtains told of an approaching storm. It came in around midnight, and although it only rocked the boat a bit and threw rain against the portholes, it kept Ronson awake for a while. He lay in his bunk, taser beneath his pillow, listening to the shrikes and the storm.

Venus was a dangerous world.

Yet the morning was calm. The rain had slackened to a mild drizzle, the sun a hot splotch half-seen through the clouds. The frogheads were croaking impatiently beside the boat when Ronson and the others emerged from the cabin. Mikhail gave chocolate bars to two of the aborigines—as before, their leader refused to accept any—while Angelo and Ronson took down the net and hoisted the anchor. Then the captain started the engine and *Aphrodite* set out again, the frogheads once more taking the lead.

The floating isles had become bigger and less far apart by then, and for the first time Ronson saw forests on the larger ones. Slickbark trees looked like palmettos but grew in dense jungle clusters, their broad trunks strangled by vines, their broad, serrated leaves casting shadows across the surrounding water.

Around mid-morning, *Aphrodite* came within sight of a larger vessel going to the other way: a lumber ship the size of a small freighter, its deck loaded with cut and trimmed tree trunks. The lumber ship blew its horn as it went by, but Angelo didn't respond to the hail.

"A yaz runner wouldn't do that," the captain explained.

"Yaz runner?" Ronson asked. "You mean, like someone who's...?"

"Out to purchase yaz, uh-huh." Angelo gave him a sidelong look. "That's what we're going to pretend to be once we get to this place... because, believe me, there ain't no way they're gonna let us live if they don't think we're here to buy dope."

Ronson was still coming to grips with this when the frogheads suddenly turned to the right and started heading for a large island only a kilometer away. As *Aphrodite* approached the island, the three men spotted thin lines of smoke rising from its forest. Angelo handed a pair of binoculars to Ronson, and through them he saw a couple boats about *Aphrodite*'s size tied up at a floating dock.

"It's a yaz camp, all right," Angelo said, then he looked off to the side. "Hey! What the hell are they doing?"

Ronson followed his gaze. The three frogheads had suddenly turned and were swimming back toward the boat. "I think they want to talk," Mikhail said.

Angelo throttled down the engines. "So talk to 'em," he muttered with an annoyed shrug.

As the boat came to idle, the Russian walked back to the stern. By then the frogheads were dog-paddling along the starboard side, their faces visible above the water. The leader warbled something to Mikhail; he listened for a few moments, then turned to Ronson.

"She says this is the place where we will find the man we are looking for," Mikhail said, "but they refuse to go any farther. They will remain here until they see us leave, then they will follow us."

Ronson was puzzled as to why the Water Folk wouldn't escort them the rest of the way to the island, but he wasn't about to argue. As the boat began moving again, he went below, where he found the taser he'd left beneath his bunk pillow. He had just slid its holster on his belt, though, when Mikhail followed him into the cabin.

"Leave that behind," the Russian said. "If the yaz croppers see you wearing it, they'll think we mean trouble."

Ronson stared at him. "Then how the hell am I supposed to rescue the kid?"

Mad Mikhail hesitated. "We will think of something," he said at last. "Let me do the talking, yes?"

Again, Ronson didn't have a choice. As the boat came closer to the island, though, he came out on deck with the taser beneath the nylon rain jacket he'd put on. When no one was looking, he carefully hid the weapon behind the net locker where it couldn't be seen yet easily reached.

Men on the island had seen *Aphrodite* coming. Two yaz croppers were waiting on the dock as the boat glided up beside it. They grabbed the lines Mikhail and Ronson tossed to them and pulled the fishing boat alongside their own craft, then a thick-set man with grey brush-cut hair rested a foot on *Aphrodite's* gunnel, arms folded across his bare chest.

"*Priv'et*," he said, gruff yet not entirely hostile. "*Kak vas tibut?*"

"Mikhail Kronow," Mad Mikhail replied. "*Vygavarti pa angliski?*"

The other Russian looked over at his companion, a younger man with a shaved head and a goatee beard. "I do, mate," he replied, an Australian accent to his voice. "So who the hell are you, eh?"

"He is *gospodin* Ronson, an American friend." Mikhail barely glanced at Ronson. "Thank you for speaking English... his Russian is very bad." The Aussie laughed but the Russian remained silent, apparently not understanding a word they were saying. "We are here to do some business, yes?"

"What sort of business?"

"I think you know what kind." A smile and sly wink. "May we speak to your leader? Someone we can...um, how do you say...negotiate, yes?"

"*Vityazkaizkornia.*" Ronson said. Mikhail gave him a sharp look, but he saw no need to dance around the subject. There was only one reason why a boat would be all the way out here. "I'm looking to buy yaz."

The Aussie looked at the older man and spoke to him in his own language. The Russian cropper studied Ronson and Mikhail for a few moments, dark eyes sizing them up. Then he slowly nodded, and the Aussie turned to the visitors. "Sure, c'mon... this way."

Ronson glanced back at the wheelhouse. Angelo was standing at the door. He shook his head, silently telling Ronson that he was going to stay behind. Ronson nodded, then followed Mikhail off the boat. With the two croppers leading the way, they walked onto the island.

vi

The ground was soft and spongy. Until he reached the crude walkway of wooden boards laid down by the croppers, Ronson's shoes sank a bit with each step he took, making squishy sounds. The forest closed in around them as he and Mikhail were led away from the dock until they couldn't see *Aphrodite* anymore, and he fought an impulse to hold his breath against a pungent reek that permeated the humid, chlorophyll-laden air. It got stronger the farther they walked, and at first he thought it came from the jungle around them, but then they reached the middle of the island and he saw what was causing it.

A clearing had been hacked out amid the trees and tangled underbrush, and it was here that the croppers had set up camp. Wooden shacks and canvas tents surrounded an open area. Nets were suspended from tall poles erected around the periphery, doubtless to ward off night shrikes but probably also to provide camouflage from any aircraft that might pass overhead. The camp had the basic amenities—a cook tent, a cluster of satellite dishes, outhouses—and might just as well have belonged to a wilderness expedition were it not for what was in its center

Vats made from discarded fuel drums had been set up above iron braziers. Brackish water slowly boiled over wood coals, emitting stinking fumes that made his eyes weep. The men and women stirring the vats wore bandanas around the lower parts of their faces, and Ronson wished he'd known enough to take the same precautions. Lumpy brown scum floated on top of the bubbling water; as he watched, one of the croppers dipped a large, long-handled spoon into a vat, carefully scooped out a dripping mass, and placed it on a tray, which was then carried to a wooden platform set up beneath a tarp and laid out to dry.

"Yaz," Mikhail murmured, nodding toward the platform.

"Yeah, here's where we make it." The Aussie—his name was Graham, Ronson had learned during the trek through the forest—proudly pointed to the vats. The Russian, whose name was Boris, had left them as soon as they entered the camp. "We drop the roots in there, boil off the resin, scoop it out, cure it... that's how we get the good stuff." His finger moved to an open-sided shed, where a couple of women were using a grocery scale to weigh bundles of *vityazkaizkornia* before wrapping them in paper and twine. "Each of those is half a kilo," Graham went on, indicating a nearby shack where a large stack of bricks could be seen through the door. "From this island alone, we'll probably get... oh, I'd say, five hundred kilos at least."

"And then you move on," Ronson said.

"Uh-huh... another island, another crop, another big pile of rubles." Graham laughed, clapped him on the back. "Your pot farmers back in the States got nothing on us. They're stuck in one place, but we're a mobile operation."

Ronson only half-listened to Graham as he searched the faces of the men and women around them, trying to spot David Henry. No one here looked like him, though, even allowing for the bandanas covering the faces of the men stirring the vats. Indeed, no one in the camp looked like they were being forced to do anything. Some smiled and joked as they worked, and there were no armed guards keeping them in line. If anyone here had been shanghaied, they didn't seem to be upset about it.

Bulgakov may have been wrong, and the frogheads... Ronson felt annoyance growing in him. How could he have been so stupid as to trust those things? Masters of the World Ocean, his soaked ass. Animals, really, despite what Mikhail claimed. No wonder he was called Mad Mikhail...

Someone tapped him on the shoulder. Ronson looked around, saw that Boris had returned. And standing beside him, wearing a jungle hat and a sweat-stained Coldplay T-shirt, was David Henry.

"Hello," David said, offering a handshake. "I hear you'd like to buy some yaz."

It was only his brief experience working undercover for the NYPD vice squad that kept Ronson from showing the surprise he felt. In an instant, he realized why David Henry had disappeared without a trace. Perhaps he hadn't come to Venus intending to become a drug lord. Perhaps the opportunity presented itself only after he'd been here a while. Yet he wasn't a captive of these yaz croppers; he was their boss.

"That's what I'm looking to do." Ronson shook his hand. "Nice little operation you've got here. Never knew how this stuff was made."

David grinned, shrugged nonchalantly. "Not many people do until they see it themselves. No harder than weed… or even crack, for that matter. And out here, it's a little easier to get away with." He motioned to the nets strung above them. "That's really just to keep out the birds. The law's just about given up trying to find us. I don't think they even give a shit anymore."

Ronson silently agreed. Bulgakov had just about told him as much. "Must be a hassle getting the roots, though," he said, trying to find something to talk about while he gave himself a chance to figure out how to play this. He looked around the camp. "I mean, it doesn't look like you're cutting down any trees."

"Well, I've got my own…" David's voice trailed off. His gaze had fallen on Mikhail, who stood quietly nearby. "Hey, I know you!" he exclaimed. "You're—" he snapped his fingers a couple of times, trying to summon a memory "—that guy! The one who hangs out on the docks in Veneragrad and gets the froggies to pose for pictures!"

"Mikhail Kronow." Mikhail's eyes shifting nervously back and forth.

"Yeah! Mad Mikhail!" David was both surprised and happy to see him. "I guess you don't remember me. We never talked or anything, but… man, do I remember you! I owe you a lot, dude!"

Mikhail stared at him. "You do?"

"Uh-huh." David looked at Ronson again. "You got him as your translator, right? I mean, he couldn't have known how to find us, so I guess the dude who's driving your boat must have done that."

"That's pretty much it, yeah." Ronson let David make his own assumptions. "Mikhail hooked us up when I told him what I was looking for, so…"

"Cool." David returned his attention to Mikhail. "Like I was saying, that trick you have? Getting the froggies to come running for chocolate?" He waved an expansive hand around the camp. "That's made all this possible. C'mon, lemme show you…"

Another boardwalk led away from the camp. It ended at a smaller clearing not far away, where two croppers stood around a hole. It appeared to have been cut straight down through the vines and moss that made up the floating island, forming a deep well. A wheelbarrow stood nearby; the two men watched the hole, as if waiting for something to emerge.

"When I first came here," David explained as they approached the hole, "croppers were using roots of slickbark trees cut down by the lumber operators. Which is okay, except that by the time our people got to them, the roots were all dried out, and that meant the yaz they got from them had lost much of its potency. Everyone knew that fresh roots make better yaz, but since slickbark roots grow underwater, you'd have to use scuba gear and trained divers to swim beneath the islands to get to them. And that's dangerous as hell… something might eat you while you're down there. Then I had an idea…"

"Coming up," said one of the men watching the well.

The water bubbled for a moment, then a froghead came to the surface. Its silver eyes regarded the men standing around the well for a couple of seconds; they stepped back from the hole to give it room, and the aborigine came the rest of the way up. A nylon bag was harnessed to its chest; once the froghead was standing on dry ground, one of the men unfastened the harness, carried the bag over to the wheelbarrow, and upended it. A couple of wet, fibrous objects that looked like large knots fell into the wheelbarrow: slickbark roots.

The man who'd collected the bag from the froghead picked up a root, inspected it, then held it out for his boss to see. He said something in Russian; David frowned a little, but nodded anyway. The other cropper reached into his pocket, pulled out a Hershey bar, and held it out to the froghead.

Surprisingly, the aborigine didn't immediately take it. "*Wurgowogkakroh*," it croaked, looking down at the hole from which it had just emerged. "*Krokkakow wok-wokka.*"

Mikhail hissed, an angry sound that only Ronson heard. He didn't say anything, but from the corner of his eye, he could see that Mikhail's mouth drew into a tight line. "Oh, c'mon," the man with the candy bar said; he was an American, a Southerner judging by his accent. "Take it and git back down there." When the froghead didn't accept the chocolate, he yanked a cattle prod from his belt. "This or this," he said, holding up both the prod and the Hershey bar. "Your choice."

The froghead flinched at the sight of the cattle prod. Ronson realized then that this creature was different from the three Water Folk who'd escorted *Aphrodite* from Veneragrad. Thinner, its head slumped forward and its eyes dulled, there were dark, bruise-like marks on its flanks which could have only been caused by electrical burns. He was looking at a slave.

"*Kroh*," it said softly, then it reached for the Hershey bar.

"Yeah, *kroh* this, you ugly mother." The cropper broke the bar in half and tossed the froghead the smaller part. "Now git back down there... and next time, make 'em bigger!"

The froghead put the chocolate in its mouth, swallowed it slowly. Then, as if resigned to its fate, it turned and jumped feet-first down the hole.

"Pretty slick," Ronson said softly. Mikhail remained quiet.

"I kinda think so." David grinned, proud of himself. "I mean, it's just regular, ordinary chocolate, but they're totally addicted to it. So all we have to do is a find a few froggies, give them a couple of bars, then don't give 'em any more until they learn to chew off slickbark roots and bring 'em to us."

"Hell, I don't think they want anything else now *but* chocolate." The man with the cattle prod started to take a bite from the other half of the bar, then stopped himself. "Running low, boss," he added, his voice becoming worried. "I don't think we've got but a few bars left."

"Really?" David frowned. "Well, we're going to have to do something about that. Next time we send someone to Veneragrad for supplies..."

"We got some on the boat," Ronson said.

"Oh, yeah?" David looked at him again, his face brightening again. "How much?"

"Whole bag full. Couple of dozen bars at least." Ronson was exaggerating—he knew that Mikhail had brought only a few—but an idea had occurred to him. "C'mon back to the boat and I'll give 'em to you. We can work out a deal on the way… I've got the cash there, too."

A smile stretched across David Henry's face. "Sounds like a plan." He turned to walk back toward the camp. "I like a man who comes prepared. Let's go."

Ronson followed him, consciously avoiding Mikhail's angry glare.

vii

Capturing David Henry was almost ridiculously easy. The kid was so confident that the Russian authorities would never catch him, he'd become trustful of anyone who offered to buy yaz from him. He didn't even take any of his crew with him when he followed Ronson and Mikhail back to the dock.

Ronson kept up the pretense on the way to the *Aphrodite*. He had to guess how much a runner might offer for a hundred kilos of yaz, but it appeared that he was close to the mark when he bid 500 thousand rubles. David tried to talk him up to 600, and by the time they reached the boat, they'd settled on 550. Plus the bag of chocolate bars, which David laughingly called "a sweetener."

He was still chuckling at his own joke when they stepped onto the boat. Ronson was smiling, too, as he casually bent down beside the net locker and found the taser he'd hidden there. He straightened up, turned around, and fired it at David before he knew what was happening. The charged prongs hit him in the chest; the kid collapsed with little more than a grunt, and he was still twitching on the aft deck when Ronson and Mikhail hastily cast off the lines and Angelo started up the engine.

By the time David regained his senses, his wrists and ankles were bound and he'd been deprived of the jackknife Ronson found in his pocket. He rolled over on the deck and glared at the detective. "What the fuck are you—?"

"Your father hired me to come find you." Ronson was sitting beneath the tarp, watching the island as it receded behind them. "If you're lucky, I'll be taking you home to him. But I know a certain cop who might have a say in that, so…" He shrugged.

"Dude, you're so screwed. When my guys figure out what you've done…"

"They'll come after you?" Ronson shook his head. "Don't count on it. No one's following us. I imagine that, even if they put two and two together, they're not going to risk everything trying to rescue you. My guess is that they'll pack up and move out as fast as they can, and someone will take over as the new boss." He glanced at David, gave him a knowing smile "Hate to break it to you, kid, but with guys like that, you're expendable. And easily replaced."

David Henry glowered, but didn't reply. He must have realized the truth of what Ronson was saying. Ronson cracked open a beer he'd found in the galley. "So how did you fall into all this, anyway? Did you come here looking to get into the yaz business, or was it just something you stumbled into and…?"

"Slow down!" Mikhail was standing at the bow, searching the waters ahead. "Stop! The Water Folk are just ahead!"

"Oh, for God's sake…" Angelo was reluctant to stop for the frogheads who'd led them to the island, but he throttled down the engines, and the boat coasted to a halt. "Make it quick, okay? I want to put distance between us and the croppers."

The three aborigines floated just beneath the surface, their protrudent eyes the only things visible. As the boat idled, its engine still throbbing, Mikhail leaned over the rail and called to them. He spoke for nearly a minute, but the frogheads didn't respond. When he was done, they silently submerged, vanishing as if they'd never been there. Angelo waited a few seconds to make sure he wouldn't run over them, then started up the boat again.

"What did you say to them?" Ronson asked once Mikhail came back to the aft deck.

Mikhail didn't reply at once. He stood over David Henry, hands clenched at his sides, regarding the kid with cold and murderous eyes. David tried to return his gaze, but quickly looked away. "I told them we found the man we were looking for," Mikhail said at last, his voice low, "and thanked them for their help."

"That's all?" Ronson didn't believe him. Mikhail had spoken a long time for something as simple as that.

Mikhail nodded, then went below, closing the cabin door behind him.

Aphrodite continued westward, chasing the shrouded sun as it gradually dipped toward the horizon. It was beginning to slide into the ocean when Angelo called a stop for the night. There were no islands around, so he simply stopped the engines, allowing the boat to drift. With no nearby islands, there was little chance they'd attract the shrikes who haunted them. The captain left the nets in the locker, and since it was a mild evening Mikhail suggested that they have dinner on the aft deck beneath the tarp.

Time to relax a bit. All the same, Ronson took the precaution of scanning the ocean with the binoculars. Aside from a distant logging ship, they'd seen no other boats since escaping the yaz camp. As he'd predicted, the croppers had apparently decided that pursuing the people who'd abducted their chief—their former chief—was more trouble than it was worth. And although he'd occasionally glimpsed Water Folk breaching the surface, they'd kept away from the boat. He couldn't tell whether they were the same ones they'd met before, but he doubted it. Their task was done; no reason for them to have anything further to do with the humans.

He was wrong.

Darkness had fallen when a froghead rose to the surface just behind *Aphrodite*'s stern. By then, the four men were seated in folding deck chairs beneath the awning. Ronson had removed the ropes around David's ankles but left his wrists tied; he was eating canned stew from the paper plate Angelo had placed in his lap when Ronson happened to glance behind the boat and spotted a pair of eyes that reflected the light of the deck lamps like silver coins.

"Company," he said.

Angelo turned around in his chair, following his gaze. "Oh, hell," he muttered, annoyed by the distraction. "What does it want?" He looked at Mikhail. "Give it a candy bar and tell it to go away. It's putting me off my food."

Mikahil had been quiet all afternoon, saying little to anyone. Now he put down his plate, pushed back his chair, and stood up. Instead of turning to the froghead—no, Ronson realized, there wasn't just one pair of eyes, but two... and now three—he looked at David.

"You remember when we were at your camp and you were showing us how you got the Water Folk to bring you tree roots?" he asked. "You remember that one of them said something to you and your people?" David said nothing, and he went on. "I know you did not understand what it was saying, but I did. It said that it did not want any more chocolate, and then it begged you to let it go."

"Yeah, well..." The kid was watching the frogheads. They were coming closer to the boat. Ronson counted six pairs of eyes, and it seemed like more were coming. "That's really tough, but I don't think... I don't think..."

"No. You don't think, do you?" Mikhail stepped away from the circle of chairs, out from under the tarp. "And now you pay the price."

A thump against the stern, then a froghead reached over the side. With surprising speed and agility, it pulled itself aboard. Its feet had barely touched the deck when another one followed it. And then a third.

"Hey, what you...?" Angelo was out of his chair, staring at the creatures. "Tell these goddamn things to get off my boat!"

"They will be gone soon." Mikhail was calm, hands at his sides. "They will leave as soon as they have taken what they want from us." A faint smile. "And no, it isn't chocolate."

"Mikhail, this has gone far enough." Ronson stood up, felt for the taser he'd clipped to his belt. His hand fell upon an empty holster. Sometime in the last half-hour or so, it had disappeared. He remembered Mikhail bumping against him just before they sat down for dinner, and immediately knew what he'd done. "Mikhail...!"

Frogheads were climbing over the starboard and port gunnels. Ronson could hear more coming over the bow. Eight, ten, twelve? He had no idea how many. Now it wasn't just their eyes which were reflecting the light, but also the teeth within their open mouths. Wet, sharp teeth...

"Get 'em away from me!" The plate fell from David Henry's lap as he leaped to his feet. His eyes, when they swung toward Ronson, were wide and utterly terrified. "Get a gun or something and get 'em the fuck away from me!"

Ronson looked at Mikhail. Frogheads were standing on either side of the Russian now, advancing toward the other three men beneath the tarp. "Don't do this. Mikhail, don't let them do this..."

"Go below," Mikhail replied. "You too, Captain. If you do not interfere, they will not—"

All at once, the Water Folk attacked.

Ronson saw little of what happened next. It was swift, it was violent, and by the time he and Angelo reached the cabin and threw themselves inside, it was over. Almost. The screams were still coming as the captain slammed the door shut and they put their weight against it.

The frogheads hadn't come for them, though. They'd come for David Henry.

And for Mikhail, too.

Both men put up a fight, but it didn't last but a few seconds. The boat rocked back and forth, and there were the sounds of a struggle from the other side of the door. A series of loud splashes. And then the night was quiet again.

Ronson waited a minute or so. Not just to make sure that the frogheads had left, but also to give his heart a chance to stop hammering against his chest. Then, with Angelo fearfully peering over his shoulder, he inched the door open and peered out.

Overturned chairs. A ripped tarp. Blood on the deck, already mixing with puddles of sea water. No bodies.

The two men stood on the aft deck, feeling the warm rain against their faces. In the far distance, lightning flashes briefly delineated the horizon, painting the clouds with shades of purple and silver, silver the color of the Water Folk's eyes. A soft rumble of thunder. A storm was approaching.

"I really hate this fucking planet," Angelo whispered.

"Yeah," Ronson said. "Me too."

EINSTEIN'S SHADOW

i

The world knew him as Dr. Einstein, the greatest mind of the 20th Century. For a couple of days in October, 1933, I knew him as Albert. Our acquaintance began as just another job, but it turned into something more than that. How could it not, when matters of women, revenge, and quantum physics were involved?

I wouldn't have gotten mixed up in the whole affair if I hadn't already been in London. The Harrell-Egan Detective Agency—my partner and I were in the New York phone book; you could find us under *Private Eyes, Gumshoes, or Goons*—had been hired to tail a wealthy young bank executive on a business trip to England. No one was worried whether he was absconding with someone else's money; he was engaged to the daughter of the bank's president, and the old man was concerned that his future son-in-law might be seeing someone else on the side—namely, the young buck's secretary, a pretty little thing considerably more attractive than his fiancé. So I booked a cabin on the First Class deck of the RMS *Aquitania*, where I could keep an eye on the two-bedroom suite they were sharing, and bribed chambermaids and porters to let me know what they were finding behind closed doors.

So far as I could tell, the father of the bride had nothing to worry about. Over the course of the next three days, my spies reported that the beau and his secretary stayed out of each other's beds, and when they were in public they behaved just the way they were supposed to, as two professionals on an overseas business trip. I went so far as to sidle up to my quarry in the first-class saloon, buy him a drink, and make some suggestive comments about his traveling companion, hinting that she might be just the sort of lady with whom he'd enjoy cuddling up on a cold night at sea. He was properly scandalized; in fact, if I hadn't hastily apologized, I might have left the bar with a bloody nose. Or, more likely, been forced to give him one… I'm not easy to hit.

By the time the two of them disembarked in Liverpool and caught a cab into London, they'd pretty much confirmed my suspicions that they were not up to no good. Even Shirley Temple would have considered them dull. I trailed them to their hotel across from Hyde Park, observed from a discreet distance in the lobby while they checked into separate rooms, then went to my slightly cheaper hotel a few blocks away and sent a cable to my client, informing him that he had nothing to worry about: our man would be a fine husband for his daughter, albeit boring as hell.

I offered to continue surveillance, but the client was satisfied by my report. Besides, keeping me on retainer was an expensive proposition, particularly considering that his bank had lately come close to shutting its doors for good. So my job was done, and I had a few days to kill before I caught another Cunard liner back to the States. I hadn't been in England since the war, though, and my expenses were paid, so I decided to play tourist for a while. My partner could take care of business until I got home.

The second night in London, I was getting ready to step out for the evening—dinner in Piccadilly, maybe a show after that—when there was a knock on the door. I hadn't ordered room service, and it was too late in the day for the chambermaid. "Who's there?"

"Mr. James Egan? May I speak with you, please?"

The voice from the other side of the door was polite and had a public-school British accent, but there was just enough of an edge to it to make me suspect that it belonged to a flatfoot. And no one calls me James, not even my mother. Had to be a cop. I opened the door a couple of inches. "Show me the tin."

A tall, stringy-looking fellow with a horse face blinked at me. "Pardon me?"

"I want to see your badge."

"How did you know I'm…?"

"Just a hunch."

He reached into his overcoat, pulled out a patent-leather badge holder, flipped it open to reveal a gold detective's shield. "Proof enough, I hope?"

"It'll do." I swung the door the rest of the way open. "C'mon in. Care for a drink?"

"Thank you, but no." My caller put his badge away and stuck out his hand. "Inspector Nigel Graham, Metropolitan Police. Mr. Egan…"

"Call me Sonny." I shook his hand. "That's how I knew you're a cop. The only way you'd be using my first name is if you've looked at my passport, and the only way you'd get to see that is if you'd shown your badge to the desk clerk and told him to fetch it from the safe."

An appreciative smile, a knowing nod. "Excellent deduction. My compliments. Care to take a crack at where I was before I came here?"

"Sorry. That's as much like Sherlock Holmes as I'm going to get." I went back to fastening my cuff links. The job had called for me to bring proper evening wear, and there was no sense in letting my penguin suit stay in my suitcase for the rest of the trip. "So, what brings you here?"

"I'd like for you to come with me," he replied, and quickly shook his head when I cast him a sharp look. "Oh no, you're not in any trouble. In fact, someone would like to speak with you about retaining your services."

"Really?" I fastened my collar and reached for my black tie. "Is there a shortage of dicks in London?"

Again, the curious look. "Oh… you mean detectives! Sorry, American slang often baffles me. No, no, Scotland Yard has no lack of plainclothes operatives. In this instance, though, we and our associates have need of someone who doesn't have any official standing… that is, who's not attached to any particular government agency, either here or in the States."

"I see." I swung the tie around my neck and began to curl it into a bow. "And who're your associates?"

"I'm not at liberty to discuss that. But I can tell you we're heading for the American embassy."

"Really?" I wasn't expecting that. Indeed, this was a new one; Harrell-Egan never had Uncle Sam as a client before. "I wasn't aware that my country held me in such high regard."

Graham sat down on the edge of my bed and waited for me to finish getting dressed. "Again, I can't tell you very much. I can inform you, though, that when the Yanks began casting about for someone on this side of the Pond to do a small errand for them, your name came up as someone considered trustworthy and reliable. You just completed an assignment, didn't you?" I nodded. "That's who recommended you… your last employer."

"Is that a fact?" My most recent client must have more pull than I thought, for the government to come to him asking for advice for good P.I.'s. "Glad to know I've scored points for customer satisfaction."

"Yes, well—" Graham glanced at his watch "—we have someone waiting for us, so if you'd kindly hurry…"

"Not a problem." I pulled on my tails, picked up my top hat and cane, checked my appearance in the mirror. I looked like a sharp-dressed young American out for a night on the town. The embassy staff better appreciate my appearance. I opened the bureau drawer and pulled out my money clip, then snagged the room key. "All set. Let's go."

Graham eyed me. "You're not carrying a gun?"

"A fan of detective stories, aren't you?" I asked, but he didn't smile. "No, I didn't bring one with me. My last job didn't call for me to carry a piece." Not to mention that the U.K. had very stringent laws regarding private handgun possession.

"Hmm." He opened the door. "Well, we'll have to do something about that. Perhaps my department can loan you a weapon."

That stopped me. "You think I'm going to need a gun?"

"It'll put quite a few people's minds at ease if you carry one, yes."

ii

The American embassy was located on Portland Place in the Marylebone district. The taxi Graham had waiting outside my hotel got us there in just a few minutes. We didn't come in through the front entrance, though, but instead entered through a side door in the alley, out of sight from the street. An embassy staffer was waiting for us; he escorted upstairs to the third floor and left us in an ordinary office with a portrait of George Washington overlooking a teak writing desk. Through tall windows, street lamps were just beginning to come on.

I was beginning to wonder who had the bright idea of hanging a picture of General Washington in the British embassy when the door opened again. The man who walked in was in his mid-fifties, trim and grey-haired. One look at my outfit, and he chuckled in a way that managed to be both friendly and condescending at the same time.

"I hope I'm not disrupting any plans you may have had for the evening." He had a Boston accent, with an affected English lilt.

"Not at all. I always dress like this." I didn't get up from my seat, as Graham had, but instead casually twirled my top hat around on the tip of my cane.

"Yes... quite." He was trying for dry British humor, but he'd probably grown up playing stickball in Southie. He couldn't think of a comeback, so he settled for offering a handshake. "Richard O'Donnell, assistant consul. And you're James Egan... or may I call you Sonny?"

"Sonny will do." I didn't trust men whose handshakes were as limp as his, but I decided to give him the benefit of the doubt. "Inspector Graham here told me how you found me, but he didn't tell me why. Want to give me the lowdown?"

O'Donnell glanced at Graham, did a double-take. "Where's the other man? The one I spoke to yesterday?"

"I've been assigned to the case," Graham replied. "The chief superintendent understands I have knowledge of this sort of thing... German intelligence operations, that is."

"Yes, of course. Very well." O'Donnell turned to me again. "If by 'lowdown' you mean an explanation..."

"I wouldn't mind getting one."

"By all means." He strolled over to a sideboard. "Drink?"

"Bourbon if you have it. Water if you don't."

"Bourbon, I have... from Kentucky, in fact. I'm afraid I've never developed a taste for Scotch." He picked up a crystal decanter and poured a couple of fingers in a pair of glasses. "What do you know about Dr. Albert Einstein? Provided that you've heard of him, of course."

He didn't really think I was an idiot, did he? I decided that I didn't like him, after all. "I've heard of him. German scientist. Said to be one of the smartest men in the world, although I'm sure there's a few poker players who'd give him a run for his money."

"If you know any card sharps who've developed something as profound as the theory of relativity, please let me know. There's certain people in our country who'd love to meet them." O'Donnell's back was turned to Graham and me as he walked behind his desk, and I took the moment to share an annoyed glance with my friend from Scotland Yard. "But, yes... Dr. Einstein is a genius, and quite a famous one at that. And he happens to be in trouble."

O'Donnell sat down at his desk, placing his drink untasted on the blotter. "As I'm certain you're aware, over the past few years there has been a change of government in Germany. The National Socialist Party—the Nazis—have come up over the past several years, and in the last election they managed to get their leader installed as president…"

"Gregor Strasser. I read the papers."

"Glad to hear it," O'Donnell replied, and I hid the look on my face by sipping my drink. It was Kentucky bourbon, all right, but the cheap kind. He probably couldn't tell the difference. "Because Strasser is less strident than the man he deposed, people think he's more liberal. Nothing could be further from the truth. Our intelligence sources doubt the allegation that Adolf Hitler shot himself, and believe instead that Strasser orchestrated a coup within the Nazi inner circle. Either way, he's is just a slicker version of the last fellow. Little has changed since he's become president, and this includes the treatment of German Jews."

"Which makes Dr. Einstein a particular target," Graham said. "He's come under attack within academic circles, with some of his detractors denouncing his work as 'Jewish science,' whatever that is. He doesn't mind confronting those chaps at all… it just gives him a chance to toy with them before swatting them down… but lately it's become more serious."

"Death threats?" I asked.

"Yes… and if the Nazis continue to crack down on the Jewish population, they probably won't be mere threats for much longer." Graham's expression was grim.

"Fortunately, Dr. Einstein is well aware of the risks he'd be taking if he stays in Germany," O'Donnell continued. "Earlier this year, he paid a visit to the United States for a speaking engagement in California. He didn't immediately return to Germany, though, but instead went first to Belgium, and then to England, where he and his wife have been house guests of an M.P. in Norfolk for the past few weeks. During this time, the Nazis seized his home and belongings, and it's pretty clear that, if he sets foot in his country again, he'll be immediately arrested."

"On what charges?"

"I don't think the Nazis need any charges," Graham said drily. "They'll arrest him for being Albert Einstein."

"He has many friends, though, and just as many options." O'Donnell picked up his drink and absently swirled it around. "He's had offers for positions at universities all over Europe, but apparently he's decided to put as much distance between Germany and himself as he can, and accepted a position at the Institute for Advanced Study in Princeton, New Jersey."

He said the last as if there was vinegar in his glass. I suppose he was disappointed that Einstein wasn't taking a job at Harvard; by then I'd noticed his class ring. "Until he actually gets to the States, though, and requests political asylum, everyone agrees it's probably best that we keep up the pretense that he's simply returning for another speaking engagement. If the Nazis were to become aware that Dr. Einstein is planning to defect, they might attempt to abduct him and bring him back to Germany."

"Or worse, liquidate him," Graham said quietly. "Anti-Semitic propaganda aside, the Nazis must be aware that losing him would be a major blow... particularly since it's becoming apparent that Strasser intends to rebuild the German war machine, and needs advanced technology to do this. If they can't have him, they may want to make sure no one can."

"So we want to get him to America as fast as possible." O'Donnell turned his chair sideways to gaze out the window behind his desk. "Dr. Einstein has agreed to this, and we're preparing to get him out of England by the next available means..."

"That would be the *Berengaria*," I said. "Leaves for New York next Thursday. I've already booked a cabin."

"No." O'Donnell shook his head. "The state department believes that the longer Dr. Einstein and his wife remain in England, the greater the chance of him being assassinated by a German agent. And even once they're aboard a ship, he won't be entirely safe. No, I'm afraid we're going to have to spirit them out of Great Britain another way... and that's aboard the *Valkyrie*."

I stared at him, not quite believing what he was saying. "The *Valkyrie* is a German aircraft. I assume you know that."

"Operated by Dornier-Luftwaffe Air Lines, which in turn is owned by the German government." Graham slowly nodded. "Yes, we're all too aware of this fact, Mr.... Sonny, sorry. But it's faster than an ocean liner."

"It's still crazy."

"Not so much as you think." There was a smug look on O'Donnell's face as he turned around again to pick up his drink. "We believe the Nazis will be less inclined to suspect that he's defecting if he and his wife are traveling to New York on their own airliner. And even if they do, with so many people aboard, an assassination would be rather difficult, don't you think?"

"I think it's the riskiest plan I've ever—"

"The *Valkyrie* stops in London on its way from Frankfurt to New York, and will depart from the Vauxhall wharf tomorrow at 1:30 P.M." O'Donnell sipped his whiskey. "Dr. Einstein and his wife Elsa have already been booked into a first-class cabin, and you've been booked into the one next to theirs."

"As their bodyguard," I said, and O'Donnell nodded. "Why me? Why not one of your people?" I crooked a thumb in Graham's direction. "Or his people, for that matter."

"Oh, I'm coming along as well," Graham said. "Not as a bodyguard, though, but as an intelligence asset. I'll be in second class, where you can find me."

"If German agents are watching Dr. Einstein, they'll recognize anyone Scotland Yard puts on him as protection," Graham said. "Same for any American military or diplomatic officials. Their presence could tip them off that a defection is taking place. But no one will recognize you, Sonny. You're unknown to them. Therefore, you'll be able to keep a discrete eye on the Einsteins while not appearing to be a bodyguard."

"You've come highly recommended from your last employer." O'Donnell put down his glass, folded his hands together in his lap. "I suppose you weren't aware that he has the ear of some rather powerful people in Washington, were you? When they put the word out that they were looking for someone in London who could take on this particular task..."

"Okay, I get it." The whiskey wasn't so bad just then. I shrugged as I polished it off. "At least I'll be going home in luxury." I paused. "You realize, of course, this isn't a volunteer effort."

O'Donnell said nothing, but instead reached into his desk, pulled out an envelope and slid it across the desk to me. "This covers half of your fee. You'll received the other half once the Einsteins arrive safely in America."

I opened the envelope, peeked inside, and did my best to not show my expression. There were enough American greenbacks in there to cover Harrell-Egan's office rent for the next few months; whatever came after that would be pure profit. "It'll do. I'll let you know if I have any additional expenses."

O'Donnell glared at me. On top of everything else, apparently he was also a skinflint. As I stood up and turned toward the tree where I'd left my hat, coat, and cane, he said, "I trust you're still not planning to go out on the town this evening."

"No. Dinner some place, then back to my room. I'll need my rest, after all."

"I wouldn't worry," Graham said. "Chances are, it'll be a quiet trip."

iii

I rendezvoused with Graham at noon the next day in the pub at Vauxhall Station, the terminus for the English leg of the *Valkyrie*'s flight. Even at midday, I could smell the nearby Thames. It's not the world's largest river, but it does set some sort of record as the most odorous. Over a ploughman's lunch and a couple of pints of Newcastle, Graham slipped a small wooden box to me beneath the table. Keeping it out of sight, I opened the box and peeked inside. Inside was a Colt .45 semi-automatic, along with an extra clip.

"Where did you get this?" I asked. Scotland Yard didn't routinely furnish its officers with high-caliber weapons.

"Our arsenal has a few American firearms on hand," Graham said quietly. "We figured this would be adequate."

I didn't want to tell him that I seldom carried a gun, and when I did it was usually a Smith & Wesson .38 snub-nosed revolver suitable for a coat pocket. "Don't worry," he added, noticing my raised eyebrow, "I brought a shoulder holster as well. We'd prefer if you went armed at all times."

I closed the box but kept it in my lap. "You said last night this'll be a quiet trip."

"Just in case." He glanced at his watch. "Best hurry. The Einsteins will be here in just a few minutes."

The sidewalk outside the station was crowded, mainly with rail passengers but also quite a few people arriving to board the *Valkyrie*. I'd stepped into the men's room and, in the privacy of a toilet stall, loaded the .45 and donned the shoulder holster. My jacket and overcoat concealed the gun well enough that no one on the sidewalk seemed to notice, but nonetheless it felt like I was carrying a cannon beneath my left armpit. I was beginning to wonder if this was really necessary when a sedan pulled up in front of the station and Graham tapped me on the arm.

"Here we go," he murmured.

We approached the car, and as we did the front passenger door opened and another man stepped out. "You're the escorts?" he asked. I nodded, and Graham flashed his badge. "All right, here he is." A quick glance about the sidewalk, then the plainclothes cop opened the sedan's rear door. A moment passed, then a short, stocky figure emerged from the back of the car.

Today, everyone knows who Albert Einstein was and what he looked like. He's become one of the most recognizable faces in history; his caricature is on bagel shops and popcorn bags and children's toys, his image so familiar that it's been debased to the point of meaninglessness. People who have no idea what $E=mc^2$ actually means immediately recognize him, although some of them would probably tell you that he invented the atomic bomb or was really a space alien.

But this was 1933, and while Einstein was famous, he wasn't yet an icon. The person who stood blinking in the midday sun of a cool London day was a middle-aged man in a rumpled black overcoat and a shapeless fedora pulled low over graying, ill-kempt hair. His bushy mustache was still dark, and while the corners of his eyes were crinkled with perpetual amusement, the rest of his face wasn't yet heavily lined. He regarded everything from beneath the brim of his hat with a certain air of bewilderment, as if he didn't quite know where he was or why he'd been brought here.

"This is not an airfield," he said, his German accent so thick I had to listen hard to understand what he said. "I was told we were going to board a plane."

The plainclothesman kept the smile on his face. "The plane you'll be using is amphibious, Dr. Einstein. It can only take off and land on water." He pointed to the nearby Vauxhall Bridge, where a broad set of stairs led down to the river. "It's moored down there. Now, if you'll let me introduce you..."

"Where is our baggage?" A plump, grey-haired woman in a cloche hat and a fur-collared overcoat crawled out of the sedan and angrily glanced about. "Our trunks, Albert's violin case... where did they go?"

"Your belongings have been brought here separately, Mrs. Einstein. They're already on the plane." Graham stepped forward to offer his hand. "Please let me introduce myself. I'm Nigel Graham, and this is Sonny Egan. We'll be accompanying you as your escorts."

"Our... escorts?" Einstein peered first at Graham, then at me. "Then you'll be traveling with us to America?"

"Yes, sir." I stood at Graham's shoulder and addressed both Einsteins. "I'll be in the cabin next to yours, and will be with you at all times. Nigel will be elsewhere on the plane."

"So you're going to be Albert's bodyguard." Elsa stared me straight in the eye. I could tell at once she was a tough old gal, accustomed to defending her husband. I didn't learn until later that she was also his cousin.

I shrugged. "Think of me as your shadow. That way you can pretend I'm not there."

A mischievous smile appeared within Einstein's mustache. "A shadow?" he asked, and I nodded. "And you're also an American?" I nodded again; that much was obvious. His gaze drifted to the open front of my overcoat, and from the slight widening of his eyes I could tell that he'd spotted the Colt. Then he looked up at me again and, in a very grave voice, whispered, "I know who you are..."

He thrust his right arm across the bottom of his face until all I could see were a pair of sharp eyes glaring at me from beneath the lowered brim of his hat. "Who knows what evil lurks in the hearts of men?" he intoned, and added a laugh very much like Orson Welles'.

"Albert! Stop that!" Elsa swatted his arm.

"Oh, I love that show." Einstein was still grinning as he lowered his arm. He took my hand. "Pleased to meet you, Mr. Egan. Call me Albert."

"All right... and you can call me Sonny." We shook on it, and I glanced at his driver. "Okay, we'll take it from here. Albert, Mrs. Einstein... this way, please."

Graham placed himself beside Elsa, and I took up position beside Albert, and the four of us began making our way through the crowd. For a minute or so, I thought we might make it to the plane without anyone catching on, but we hadn't even reached the steps when a taxi screeched to a halt at the curb. The doors opened and, like clowns from a circus car, a half-dozen or so reporters fell over one another in their mad scramble to be the first one out. They spotted us in an instant, and before Graham and I could do much about it, the Einsteins were surrounded by men with cameras and notebooks.

"Dr. Einstein, are you leaving England?"

"Are you moving to America? Is it permanent?"

"What do you think of Strasser?"

"Al! Hey, Al... *smile!*"

Albert looked at the Speed Graphic camera being thrust in his face and insolently stuck out his tongue. The bulb flashed, and then I pushed the photographer aside before he could get a shot of Albert giving him a rude gesture. Elsa, on the other hand, was lapping it up; she beamed at the cameras like a starlet on the red carpet, and I think she would have stopped and given an interview right there on the spot if Graham and I hadn't been present.

But the reporters weren't the worst of it. Until they showed up, no one at Vauxhall Station had recognized Einstein; he was just a little, grey-haired Jewish man with his frumpy wife, being led to the wharf by a couple of young men who might have been their sons or nephews. At the sound of his name, though, people turned to look... and within seconds, the reporters were outnumbered by men, women, and children pressing in upon us from all sides, with everyone yelling Albert's name, shoving forward hands for him to shake, pieces of paper for him to autograph, babies for him to kiss...

"Oh, dear," Albert murmured, his voice almost lost beneath the cacophony. "This isn't what I wanted."

Neither did I. In terms of security, it was a nightmare. The faces around us were smiling, happy, and excited, but any one of those hands could just as well be holding a gun or a knife. From the edge of the crowd, I heard a police whistle. Looking around, I spotted a bobby helmet. But it was too far away and the crowd was too dense. We had to get out of there.

"Grab hold of my arm," I said to Albert. He nodded and did as I asked, and I repeated the same instruction to Elsa. Graham caught on; he linked arms with Elsa, and then the four of us, like a Broadway chorus line, began marching forward in lockstep, with Graham and I raising our arms to gently but firmly push people away. The bobby caught up with us; whistle in his mouth and nightstick extended, he got in front and plowed through the mob, unapologetically shoving aside press and public alike.

We'd almost reached the top of the stairs, where a gate had been set up to check the tickets of departing Dornier-Luftwaffe passengers, when my roving eye spotted a young woman standing at the edge of the crowd. In her early thirties, dark-haired and olive-skinned, stocky and yet attractive in a bohemian sort of way, she had the exotic looks of someone of ethnic European heritage. My gaze might have passed over her in an instant were it not for one thing: the intense hatred with which she regarded Einstein, the utter scorn that stood in contrast to the wonder and joy of everyone else around us.

If she was any closer, I thought, *I'd be watching her hands.*

She stayed where she was. Our eyes met for an instant, though, and she quickly looked away. I darted a glance at Albert—apparently he hadn't noticed her, for there was an amused and unworried grin on his face—and when I looked around again, the young woman had disappeared.

Well, okay. So everyone in the world doesn't love Albert Einstein. If I could just get him to the good ol' U.S. of A., we'd be leaving a lot of those people behind. Then Herr Strasser and his minions could rant about Jewish scientists all they wanted.

Finally, we reached the stairs. Graham and I handed the tickets to a smiling young man with perfect Aryan looks standing behind a lectern marked with the winged Dornier-Luftwaffe logo. He checked our tickets and tore away the top page of each, then wished us a pleasant trip ("Why, thank you," said Albert) before letting us pass through the gate. The bobby held back everyone who wasn't holding up a ticket, and we left the crowd behind and began to walk down the stairs to the plane.

At this point, I thought our troubles were over. I had no way of knowing that they'd only just begun.

iv

The Dornier-Luftwaffe RF-01 is long gone, of course. Although the *Valkyrie* was meant to be the first of a fleet of *Riesigeflugzeuge*, it was the only one of its kind. The *Valkyrie* exists today only in photographs, newsreel footage, and the fading memories of those alive today who still remember it. It was too big to build, too expensive to operate, too much ahead of its time... and that's too bad. It was an impressive machine.

Seen from the stairs leading down to the wharf, the *Valkyrie* resembled an enormous silver boomerang mounted atop two giant pontoons, with a smaller boomerang on top of the first. The airliner took the form of a giant wing with a span of 528 feet; from the forward bow to the rear tips of its catamaran pontoons, it was 235 feet long, and from the waterline, it was as tall as a nine-story building.

But those are just statistics. Let's put it another way: it was *huge*.

The *Valkyrie* floated on the Thames below Vauxhall Bridge because this was the only place in the metropolitan London area where it could land; no airfield in the world could accommodate an aircraft that size. All landings, in fact, were on rivers—the Main in Frankfurt, the Hudson in New York. Although the *Valkyrie* was a flying ocean liner, its twenty 1,900 horsepower engines were vulnerable to salt corrosion. These three-blade prop engines were mounted on both sides of the upper nacelle: ten forward, ten aft, in a push-pull configuration.

The American architect Norman Bel Geddes and German aeronautical engineer O.A. Keller had designed the *Valkyrie* to meet the challenge of providing non-stop transatlantic passenger air travel, specifically between London and Chicago. Unfortunately, they proposed their airliner just before the New York stock market crashed; the group of Chicago businessmen who'd been interested in building the ship backed away when it became apparent that they'd soon be selling apples from pushcarts on Michigan Avenue. The airliner might have remained on Bel Geddes' drawing board if Gregor Strasser's second in command, Hermann Goering, hadn't heard about it. A former World War I flying ace, Goering had an intense interest in aeronautics, and he managed to persuade *der führer* to invest in the project as an alternative to the giant passenger dirigibles proposed by Count von Zeppelin. Since the dirigibles were dependent on hydrogen for lift, the Bel Geddes airliner was considered a safer design.

Not to mention more adaptable for military use. As Graham and I escorted Albert and Elsa across the wharf to the floating pier leading out to the *Valkyrie*'s port pontoon, I couldn't help but wonder if there were plans for conversion of a civilian airliner to a military troop ship. Five decks of portholes ran the length of each of the pontoons and three decks of the main hull; the *Valkyrie* had accommodations for 451 passengers and 155 crewmembers, and it wasn't hard to imagine them replaced by an invasion force of the same size.

Of course, that was a silly thought. Strasser had repeatedly stated that the Nazis wanted only peace. Still, it was hard to ignore the bright red swastika painted on the hull. And when the war finally did break out, one of the first targets for British air raids was the *Valkyrie*'s hanger in Frankfurt.

"Have you ever seen anything so enormous?" Elsa stopped midway across the wharf to crane her head back and peer up at the vast wing looming above us. "Albert, this is the biggest thing I've ever seen."

"Hmph... the Eiffel Tower is bigger." Albert took off his hat and shaded his eyes against the sunlight glaring off the *Valkyrie's* fuselage. "Couldn't they have accomplished the same thing with a smaller aircraft?"

"Oh, you..." Elsa gave her husband a sour look. "No imagination."

"Yes, my darling. As you say." Albert gave me a sidelong look, and I tried not to smile when he winked at me. "Come, my dear... our behemoth awaits."

Two booths were set up on the pier in front of the gangways: one for First Class passengers, the other for everyone else. Graham stayed with us until we joined the line for the first-class booth, but no sooner had he walked away to join the second line than a young British officer in a dark blue Dornier-Luftwaffe uniform stepped from behind the booth and walked over to us. There were lieutenant's bars on his shoulder boards, and the embroidered patch above his left pocket was stitched OSWALD.

"Dr. Einstein? Mrs. Einstein?" He ignored me. "Please come this way. We've been expecting you."

Albert blinked, and Elsa nervously took his arm. "I'm sorry," he said, "but I don't understand. Who...?"

"Is there a problem, Lieutenant?" I asked, stepping forward.

Oswald regarded me as if I'd just crawled out from under the bridge. "Are you accompanying them?" he asked. I nodded, and he gave me a frosty smile. "Their accommodations have been changed. Compliments of the captain, they're to be moved from First Class section on Deck Seven to the Master Suite on Deck Eight."

"Oh, my... really?" Elsa raised an eyebrow. "I didn't realize Dornier-Luftwaffe took such good care of its passengers."

"Particularly Jews," Albert quietly added.

Elsa shushed him. Oswald did a good job of pretending not to notice. "Captain Schumann is an admirer of yours, Dr. Einstein. It is an honor to have you aboard the *Valkyrie*, and he wants to make your trip as comfortable as possible. Your belongings have already been taken there."

"Thank you," Albert said. "And our companion, Mr. Egan? Where will he...?"

"Mr. Egan will continue to enjoy our hospitality on the First Class deck." He looked at me. "I'm sorry, sir, but the Master Suite has only one bedroom, and the *Valkyrie* doesn't provide roll-away beds for its guests."

I didn't like it. My instructions were to stick with Albert and Elsa at all times. This looked like a deliberate attempt to separate us. Yet there was little I could do about it without revealing that I was their bodyguard, and therefore tipping off the Nazis that Albert was, indeed, planning to defect.

Albert and I traded a silent glance, and he gave me the slightest of nods. We'd work something out once we were airborne. "Thank you, Lieutenant," he said. "We accept your invitation. Elsa, Sonny..."

Oswald wasn't pleased that I was coming aboard with them, but he didn't want to risk offending Albert, so he had little choice but let me fall in behind the Einsteins as he led them around the line of First Class passengers. I caught a glimpse of Graham standing in line with the Second and Third Class passengers. His face displayed no expression as our eyes briefly met, but I could tell that he'd overheard the conversation and was just as concerned as I was.

And the girl I'd spotted on the sidewalk was there, too. Standing near the back of Graham's line, she quickly looked away when I spotted her. She pretended to examine the ticket in her hand, but it was clear that she'd been quietly watching as well. Maybe she was just a Strasser sympathizer who had a grudge against Albert, but...

In any case, I pegged her as someone worth keeping an eye on.

v

We entered the RF-01 through a passenger hatch on Deck Two, amid a row of small, double-occupancy Third Class cabins at the waterline of the port pontoon. Stairs led upward, but Oswald took us instead to an elevator midway down the corridor. Its operator closed the grate behind us; he pulled up the control wheel, and the elevator quietly ascended.

As we rose through the airliner, passing from the pontoon into the center hull of the immense wing, we caught brief glimpses of the rest of the ship—the lower passenger decks, the foyer leading to the main dining room, the entrance to the solarium and games court, the promenade and First Class cabins—until we reached Deck Eight, the airliner's highest level besides the engine nacelle above us.

"And here we are," Oswald said as the operator brought the cage to a halt and opened the door. The lieutenant led us down a narrow carpeted hallway past the officer's quarters on the right, pausing for a moment at a large door to our left. "This is the control room. Once you've been shown your quarters, Captain Schumann would be pleased if you'd join us for the take-off."

"We'd be delighted," Albert said.

"And where will I be staying?" I asked

"We have a stateroom reserved for you just downstairs." Oswald pointed to a nearby companionway. "If you take those down one flight, your room is the second to the right."

Bad arrangement. It put me too far away from the Einsteins. I said nothing, though, as I followed them and Oswald a few more steps down the corridor, where he stopped to unlock an unmarked door next to the captain's quarters. We walked into a two-room suite not much larger than an ordinary bedroom, yet as modernly furnished in the Art Deco style as the most luxurious Manhattan hotel. A floor-to-ceiling window took up an entire wall of the parlor; we were high atop the airliner, looking down from the port bow upon the busy Thames, where police boats were clearing river traffic from the mile-long stretch between the Vauxhall and Chelsea bridges.

One look, and Elsa moaned and rushed into the adjacent bedroom. Albert quietly tutted and followed her, but not before he paused at the window to hastily close the drapes. "Is there anything wrong, Dr. Einstein?" Oswald asked.

"Nothing to worry about," Albert replied. "Our bags are here, yes?"

That was obviously not the reason why Elsa fled the room, but the lieutenant didn't press the issue. Albert hastily went after his wife, and I was taking note of the fact that the parlor had a sofa just big enough for me to sleep on when a telephone on the coffee table rang. Oswald picked it up, listened for a moment. "Yes, sir, we'll be there soon. Thank you." He hung up and turned to Albert, who'd just stuck his head through the door. "That was the captain. We'll be departing in ten minutes. Dr. Einstein, Mrs. Einstein, if you'd care to follow me…?"

"I would prefer to remain here, if you don't mind," Elsa said from the next room.

Glancing past Albert, I saw that she'd already removed her hat and shoes and was stretched out across the bed, an arm thrown over her eyes. Albert gave me an apologetic look. "Heights and air travel don't suit her very well, I'm afraid. I think it's better if we remain here…"

"No, Albert… go, go." Still covering her eyes, she flapped a hand at her husband. "You're expected, and it would be rude if you didn't. I'll be fine. Take Sonny with you."

I was glad she'd said that. It meant that I was taking her place, and therefore wouldn't have to argue with Oswald if the lieutenant objected. But Oswald didn't seem to mind. "Yes, ma'am. I'll have the ship's doctor come up once we're underway to see how you're doing. In the meantime… gentlemen, this way, please?"

He led Albert and me back down the corridor, where another key opened the door to the control room. We entered a compartment about the size of a steamship bridge, V-shaped with broad windows on either side of the delta. The pilot, co-pilot, and navigator were seated beneath the windows; the flight engineer and radio operator had their own stations behind them, and in the center of the compartment was the captain's chair, situated so that he could swivel in any direction.

As we came in, the captain turned about to face us. "Ah… Dr. Einstein!" A short, wiry man in his mid-30s, he stood up to thrust forward his hand. "A pleasure to meet you. I'm Max Schumann, Captain of the *Valkyrie*."

"A pleasure to meet you as well, *herr kapitan*." Einstein shook his hand guardedly. Apparently he'd noticed the same thing I had: a small red Nazi Party button on his lapel.

If the captain had any misgivings about having a Jewish scientist aboard his aircraft, though, I couldn't tell. Schumann took Albert around the control room, introducing him to each of his officers, all of whom greeted him just as enthusiastically as Schumann had. While this was going on, Oswald ducked outside again, returning a few minutes later with a white-jacketed steward carrying a pair of folding aluminum-frame chairs. They were set up against the rear bulkhead where they wouldn't tip over when the *Valkyrie* took off. Schumann made sure we were comfortable, then returned to his seat.

By then, the river had been cleared of all boats and barges. On the other side of the Thames, a large crowd had gathered along Grosvenor Road, waiting to see the *Valkyrie* take flight. The co-pilot reported that all passengers and crew were aboard and that the hatches were secure, and the engineer stated that each of the engines had been tested and were ready for full start. A final radio test, then Captain Schumann ordered the dock to be withdrawn and the aircraft to be towed to position.

"Mind if I smoke, Captain?" Albert asked.

Schumann glanced over his shoulder at him. Albert already had his briar pipe and tobacco pouch out and was gazing at him expectantly, "No… not at all," he said, even though there was a *Rachen Verboten* sign on the bulkhead above Albert's head that he couldn't have missed seeing. "Be my guest."

Albert nodded, smiled, and stuffed his pipe. The tobacco he smoked would have felled an ox at twenty paces. It didn't bother me much, but I saw the captain wrinkle his nose. Albert glanced at me and gave me a sly wink. Yes, he'd seen the sign. He was doing this deliberately.

The first sensation of movement came a minute later, when a tugboat began dragging the *Valkyrie* by its forward mooring line away from the wharf, while tenders on both the port and starboard sides helped push the giant aircraft to its take-off position, in the center of the river and facing directly downstream. From the control room, much of London's southwest side could be seen, from Victoria Station to Buckingham Palace, all the way out to the Royal Albert Hall and the green space of the Kensington Gardens.

As the tug and tenders began to move away, Schumann picked up a microphone and had the radio operator put him on the ship's speakers. Speaking first in German, then in English, he asked all passengers to be seated and remain that way until told that it was all right to move about the aircraft. He put away the mike and, speaking in German, told the pilots to start the engines.

It took *Valkyrie* nearly the entire length of the river between the two bridges to become airborne. Moving slowly at first, but building speed with each passing second, the giant aircraft rushed down the Thames, its mammoth pontoons sending dovetails of water high into the air, its twenty engines moaning loudly even through the soundproofed fuselage. Because the Thames had a shallow bend in this part of the river, *Valkyrie* came close first to one bank, then another.

As the Chelsea Bridge became steadily larger, I saw Albert balling his fists in his lap, the pipestem clenched between his teeth. I couldn't blame him. The take-off was tight, with no room for error.

And yet, seemingly at the last possible moment, the pontoons lifted away from the river, and the prow titled back in plenty of time to clear the bridge. A last, brief glimpse of London, then the colossus rose into the sky, the sun glaring through the windows as the RF-01 veered slightly starboard, making a gradual turn to the northwest. Then it leveled off and continued its long ascent to 10,000 feet, where it would remain for the next thirty-three hours of its transatlantic flight.

Albert was grinning like a kid. He knocked out his pipe over a waste can, thanked Schumann for inviting him to witness the take-off—"I'll never forget this for as long as I live!"—and then he let Oswald escort him back to his cabin. I was about to follow him in, but the lieutenant tapped me on the shoulder.

"Perhaps you'd like to see your stateroom, sir," Oswald said. "You can come back to see Dr. Einstein any time after that."

I didn't intend to spend a lot of time in my cabin, but for the sake of appearances at least, I needed to go along with him. So I let Oswald lead me downstairs to Deck Seven, which stretched the entire length of *Valkyrie*'s hull. My room was farther away than he'd led me to believe; as we walked down the promenade, passing First Class passengers standing at the railing to watch the English countryside below, I couldn't help but again suspect that someone was making an effort to separate Albert Einstein from his traveling companion.

That was confirmed as soon as Oswald unlocked the door to my stateroom and stepped aside. There was already someone in the room, a man in a black leather overcoat who stood up from a chair as I walked in.

"You are James Egan?" he asked, his voice thickened by a German accent. "Very good. My name is Hans Lentz, and I am with the German state police."

vi

Lentz could have come straight from a Hitchcock film: tall, trim, and hawk-faced, his head shaved at the sides and back so that only the top of his scalp was covered by black hair. I didn't have to ask how he knew my name or how he'd gotten into my quarters; anyone who read the papers knew about the *Geheime Staatspolizei*—the Gestapo—recently formed to enforce the Fatherland's increasingly stringent laws. The only question was why he was here.

"Yeah, I'm Egan." I didn't tell him that my friends call me Sonny; he was clearly not my friend. "Sorry, but I think you're in the wrong room."

"No, I think not." Lentz looked past me at Oswald, cocked his head toward the hall. The lieutenant said nothing, but instead stepped back from the door and quietly closed it, leaving us alone. "On this aircraft, I can go where I please."

"Really? Well, the engines could probably use another inspection. Why don't you go up there and have a look?"

No smile. He glanced over at my bed. My suitcase lay on top of it, unlatched; apparently he'd taken the liberty of searching it. "I have reason to believe you may be carrying a firearm. If that is so, I want to see it."

There was no point in denying what he already knew. I opened my coat and showed him the Colt slung beneath my left arm. "Give it to me," Lentz said, holding out his hand. "It is forbidden for passengers to carry weapons aboard German aircraft."

"Is that so?" I made no move to surrender the Colt. "Well, this may be a German aircraft, but we're over Great Britain, and there's no English law that says I can't bring a gun on a plane."

I was bluffing; I didn't know anything of the kind. But I was betting that Lentz didn't either. Apparently I'd assumed correctly. His hand clenched into a fist, then he slowly lowered it. "I do not appreciate your lack of cooperation, Herr Egan."

"And I don't appreciate you entering my cabin and going through my stuff, Herr Lentz, so let's just call it even." Figuring that it might be wise to defuse the situation, I tried a different tack. Shrugging off my overcoat and throwing it on the bed, I reached into my pocket and pulled out a pack of Camels. "Want to tell me what this is all about?" I asked, shaking out a cigarette for myself before offering one to him.

Lentz eyed the pack suspiciously before accepting a smoke. "You're accompanying Professor Einstein and his wife, are you not?" he asked, and I nodded. "May I inquire about the nature of your relationship?"

I took my time lighting my cigarette and his, then took a seat on the bed. "Old friend of the family."

Lentz sat down again, saying nothing but simply regarding me with cool appraisal. He held his cigarette between his thumb and index finger, like a kid who'd learned how to smoke just yesterday; I don't think it was something he did very often, because he didn't inhale all the way and his face looked a bit green. Still, he managed not to cough, I'll give him that.

"Old friend of the family," he said after a moment, repeating what I'd told him. "I think not. I think you are actually a bodyguard."

"You can think what you like. You're still not getting my gun."

The faintest hint of a smile, then he took one more puff from his cigarette before stubbing it out in the small glass ashtray on the table. "Perhaps we should... um, get things straight, yes? Is that the proper American phrase?"

"Close enough." He must have seen a few of our movies. "Go on."

"Very well... let me assure you that Professor Einstein and his wife are not in danger so long as they're aboard this ship. My government suspects that they may be going to America this time not merely for a visit, but permanently." A pause. "Is this true?"

"I have no idea."

"If it is, then we have no interest in standing in the way. Quite the opposite, in fact. Einstein leaving Germany just means there is one less Jew in the Fatherland. Good riddance."

"Interesting way of putting that."

Another smirk. "Mr. Egan, if I had any interest in returning Einstein to Germany, all I would have to do is instruct Captain Schumann to turn the *Valkyrie* around and fly back to Frankfurt. He could always claim engine trouble, and my people would put the Einsteins under arrest as soon as we've landed." He shook his head. "I am not going to do that. America can have them, and as many other Jews as they want."

"I'll let President Roosevelt know that the next time I see him."

Lentz stared at me as if he didn't know whether to take me seriously or not. Either way, he decided to let it pass. He got up from the chair. "Since I have let you know where we stand, you are now aware that it is not needed to guard Professor Einstein, and therefore your weapon is unnecessary. This being the case, I must request that you keep your gun in your cabin. If I see it on your person again, I will summon the stewards and have them remove it from you… by force, if required."

I didn't say anything, but simply nodded as I stood up. Lentz got the message. "Very well, then," he said as he walked toward the door. "*Auf Wiedersehen.*"

"Yeah. Nice day to you, too." I opened the door and let him out, and closed it behind him. As an afterthought, I took the chair and propped it at an angle beneath the knob. If I couldn't lock the door against him, at least I could make it difficult for him to get back in.

I should have felt a little better, now that I'd been told that the Nazis didn't care whether or not Albert defected to America, but I didn't. That would have meant trusting a Gestapo officer, and I wasn't ready to do that. My job hadn't changed. It just meant that I couldn't carry my gun, that's all.

I smiled. Lentz had forbidden me from wearing my gun in my holster. He hadn't said anything about putting it in the Einsteins' suite where I could get to it when I slept on their sofa. Which was what I intended to do until we got to New York.

vii

With that thought in mind, I went back upstairs to Deck Eight. Albert answered my knock at the door with a finger raised to his lips; Elsa was napping in the next room, and he was passing the time until dinner with his pipe and a book. He closed the bedroom door and listened while I quietly told him about my encounter with Lentz. Albert was relieved that the Nazis apparently had no interest in repatriating him to Germany, but agreed that we shouldn't take Lentz's word at face value. I'd stick with him and Elsa for the remainder of the flight, even if it meant sharing their suite overnight. However, his brow furrowed when I removed the Colt from my shoulder holster and kneeled down to slide it beneath the sofa.

"What's the Shadow without his gun?" he asked.

I chuckled at this, but he had a point. "Guess I'll have to rely on charm," I replied. "If Lentz catches me with this, he'll take it away. Maybe throw me in the brig, too, if this bird has one."

"It's certainly big enough." Albert picked up a booklet gold-stamped with the Dornier-Luftwaffe logo and a silhouette of the *Valkyrie*. "Do you know this aircraft even has a games court? And at night it doubles as a music hall?"

"Why, are you interested?"

Albert opened the booklet and peered at it. "Tonight, the Brandenburg String Quartet will be performing a selection of Mozart. It would be a pleasant way to spend the evening." He glanced about the stateroom. "And I imagine even these quarters will become a bit stale if we spend the entire trip in them."

"Then we'll go. I'll see about reserving some good seats." I made sure the gun couldn't be spotted by any casual visitors before I got up from the floor. "I'll be back before dinner. Don't go anywhere without me."

"Never." He picked up his book—*The World Set Free* by H.G. Wells—and, after a moment's absent-minded search, found his pipe where he'd left it smoldering on the coffee table. "I shall remain here till I see the whites of your eyes."

I left and went back downstairs, this time all the way down to Deck Four in the starboard pontoon where Graham was staying. I hadn't yet made it down there, though, when I found him coming up the stairs from Second Class. He was meaning to find me, believing that the Einsteins and I were still quartered together in First Class. I let him know about the new arrangements and how we'd been separated. We needed to talk, but not in his room: he was sharing a cabin with a Berlin businessman who was an enthusiastic supporter of Herr Strasser and his policies.

I wasn't sure about my room either—Lentz might have done something else in there beside search my belongings—so we went upstairs to Deck Five. Just forward of the foyer was a broad, wedge-shaped passenger lounge, where leather couches and loveseats faced the row of windows at the bow. By then, *Valkyrie* had left the Irish coast behind and was out over the ocean. With its engines throttled back to 90 mph, the enormous aircraft was chasing the afternoon sun, the long journey through the night still a few hours away.

We found a couple of armchairs off to the side, and Graham beckoned a steward and asked him to fetch a couple of drinks from the bar. Around us, passengers were watching the ocean, reading newspapers, chatting amongst themselves. A little boy ran by, holding aloft a tin-toy replica of the RF-01; he nearly collided with a young couple in tennis togs passing through the lounge on their way to the games court. Which reminded me…

"Albert wants to go to the concert tonight," I said. "I wonder who I have to see about reservations?"

It was a casual comment, but Graham shook his head. "No. They should remain in their cabin at all times."

"Why? I don't see the harm in letting them be seen in public." I pointed to the pair of double-doors behind us; they lead to the main dining room, just forward of the games court. "Dinner and a show… what could be more normal?"

"They could become targets."

"For who? The Gestapo?" I reiterated my conversation with Lentz. "I don't trust him either," I finished, acknowledging the skeptical look Graham gave me, "but I don't think he's going to try anything while dozens of people are…"

"The Gestapo isn't the only thing we need to look out for." Graham bent a little closer, lowering his voice so as not to be overheard. "There's an individual aboard who may pose a threat. Someone who's not… that is, someone who may not necessarily be affiliated with the secret police."

I don't like it when people hide important information from me, and Graham was being just a little too mysterious for my taste. "Look," I said, unable to keep the irritation from my voice, "if Scotland Yard knows something I should know, I'd appreciate it if you'd let me in on it."

Graham's lips drew together in a tight line. There was definitely something he was reluctant to reveal. One look at my face, though, told him that he wasn't getting out of here until he spilled the beans. "Very well," he said reluctantly, "there's a woman aboard who means to do harm to Dr. Einstein"

I remembered the face I'd seen in the crowd at Vauxhall Station and again on the dock just before we boarded. "Young lady? Dark hair, early thirties, kind of intense?"

"You've seen her?"

"Just before we came aboard. Want to tell me who she is?"

"Her name is Lieserl… Lieserl Maric." Graham looked about to make sure we weren't being overheard. The steward was returning with our drinks. Graham waited until he placed them on the table before us and I'd signed for them, and it wasn't until we were alone again that the inspector continued. "She's Serbian, and we have reason to believe that she bears a grudge against Dr. Einstein."

"What sort of—?"

"Never mind. It's not important." Graham shook his head. "What is important is that she must be kept away from them. If she's on the plane, it can only be because she has bad intentions."

Remembering the way she'd been staring at Albert, I couldn't argue. "Very well, then—" I picked up my scotch and water, took a sip just so it wouldn't go to waste, and started to get up "—I'll go warn Albert that—"

"*No!*"

Graham grabbed my wrist and yanked me back into my seat. Before I could argue, he leaned in, close enough that I couldn't help but see the fear in his eyes. "Whatever you do, " he hissed, "you must *not* tell Dr. Einstein or his wife that Lieserl is aboard, or even that you know her name! Do you understand?"

"What are you—?"

"*Do you understand?*"

Until then, my impression of Nigel Graham was that he was the sort of detective one finds in any police department, the kind who rise through the ranks not by wearing out shoe leather but by kissing up to his superiors so he can get the cushy assignments like shepherding German scientists across the Atlantic. In that moment, though, there was something about him that made me not only reconsider my opinion, but also wonder…

"Sure. Whatever you say." I forced a grin, playing the dumb gumshoe willing to do what he was told so long as there was a paycheck at the end of it. "Mum's the word."

"Right." Graham relaxed, letting go of my wrist as he settled back in his chair. "Sorry to be so… well, surely you understand there's certain things about this affair that can't be discussed." He seemed to remember his martini, because he picked it up and took a small taste. "Just do your job and watch the Einsteins, and I'm sure this flight will be nice and uneventful."

I nodded and made small talk with him while I finished my drink. Then I looked at my watch, commented that I still needed to make dinner reservations, and excused myself. It took just a few minutes to reserve a table for Albert, Elsa, and me during the last seating. All the seats for the evening concert had already been taken, but a flash of green and the casual mention of Albert's name was sufficient to persuade the concierge to move three First Class passengers to the waiting list.

But my work wasn't done yet.

I went up a couple of decks to the radio room and had the wireless operator send a telegram to Richard O'Donnell, he with the bad taste in Kentucky bourbon who resided at the American embassy in London.

Until a few minutes ago, I'd had no doubts about Graham. He'd shown me his shield, and as a former cop myself, I wasn't inclined to question the legitimacy of a fellow lawman. Something about him had begun to rub me the wrong way, though, and I'd just realized a peculiar thing: O'Donnell hadn't recognized Graham when he brought me to the embassy, and neither had the Scotland Yard driver who'd delivered the Einsteins to Vauxhall Station.

So I sent O'Donnell a cable:

> PLEASE CONFIRM WHEREABOUTS OF MET
> INSPECTOR NIGEL GRAHAM STOP IS HE
> ABOARD MY FLIGHT QUESTION STOP
> URGENT STOP

I watched the operator key it into his wireless, then went back to my cabin, took off my shoes, and lay down for a little while. I knew I should be with the Einsteins, but I wanted to be alone until I got a response. I could only hope that O'Donnell would take me seriously.

Apparently he did. It took a little while, but the sun was just beginning to paint red the high clouds upon the western horizon when I was awakened by a knock at the door. A steward was waiting outside, a sealed envelope resting on the silver platter he carried. I tipped him and took the envelope into my cabin, where I ripped it open and read the telegram O'Donnell had just sent me:

> CHECKED WITH MET STOP GRAHAM NOT
> ASSIGNED TO CASE STOP HE IS A TRAFFIC
> COP IN MAYFAIR STOP WHO IS WITH
> YOU QUESTION STOP

Good question, indeed.

viii

The games court was located aft of the Main Dining Room, in the solarium built within *Valkyrie*'s tail section. During the last seating of dinner, stewards moved in and cleared away the tennis equipment, badminton nets, and shuffleboards, rolled carpets across the parquet floor, and set up rows of folding chairs in front of a small, elevated stage, with a handful of upholstered armchairs in the first row. By the time dessert and coffee were being served, the solarium had been transformed into an airborne concert hall.

A couple of hours earlier, Albert, Elsa, and I had joined the rest of the rest of the First Class passengers for the last seating. I was glad I'd brought formal wear on this trip. Albert had, too, but while I looked like I might be wearing a bullet-proof vest under my tails, Albert was unexpectedly dapper. As it turned out, the reservations I'd made were redundant: at Captain Schumann's insistence, we joined him at his table, in the middle of the dining room where everyone could see us. By then, everyone aboard was aware that Albert Einstein was on their flight; all eyes were upon them the moment they walked into the dining room, and it wasn't until Schumann called for Oswald and asked him to stand behind Albert's chair that the other passengers were dissuaded from coming over for handshakes and autographs.

Unlike the scene at Vauxhall Station earlier in the day, this time the situation was under control. Albert didn't wallow in the attention, but neither did he appear to mind it very much. He'd become comfortable with celebrity, accepting it as inevitable, and his presence had an effect on people that was sometimes subtle. When we came to the captain's table, one of the first things I noticed was that the Nazi button was missing from Schumann's uniform.

Albert noticed this, too. "So, *herr kapitan*," he said once we'd been seated, "I take it you've reconsidered your political affiliation since the last time we saw one another?"

Schumann's expression became stony. There was a twinkle in Albert's eye as he said this; I was coming to realize that impudence was part of his personality. Schumann might be one of his admirers, the anti-Semitic policies of the Nazis notwithstanding, but the jab was irresistible.

"If you're speaking of my National Socialist button," Schumann said, "I'm afraid I forgot to wear it this evening. Shall I return to my cabin and retrieve it?"

"Oh, please don't," Albert replied. "Not on my account."

Elsa swatted his wrist. I found the linen napkin in my nap and coughed into it to hide my laughter. I was very glad Lentz wasn't at the table. He might have reconsidered his promise to leave Albert alone on his way to America.

But the Gestapo officer was nowhere to be seen, and neither was Nigel Graham, the man I now knew to be an imposter. I didn't tell the Einsteins what I'd learned when I came to their cabin to pick them up for dinner, but when Albert stepped into the bedroom to help Elsa fasten her pearl necklace, I took the opportunity to retrieve the Colt from beneath the sofa. The necessity of formal evening wear had given me a new place to hide my gun: in the garter strap of my right leg, where it was concealed by the trouser cuff. Not the best place for a concealed weapon, but the fact that Graham wasn't who he'd said he was had made me just as suspicious of him as anyone else aboard the *Valkyrie*.

Yet Graham didn't appear for dinner, nor did Lieserl Maric. I spent dinner watching everyone who entered the dining room, but neither of them made an appearance. I was beginning to think the evening would pass uneventfully when Albert muttered something in disgust. It was in German, but it sounded like a curse.

"Pardon me, *herr doktor*?" Captain Schumann broke away from chatting with Elsa. "Is there something wrong?"

Albert didn't say anything, but instead cast an angry glare at the orchestra balcony overlooking the dining room. The quartet who would be performing later that evening was playing a medley of Strauss waltzes for the dinner hour, and while they sounded perfectly fine to me, something about them had raised Albert's ire.

"The violinist doesn't know his instrument very well," he grumbled. "I could saw wood better than that."

I've always been more of a jazz man myself. To me, all string quartets sound like old guys sawing wood. Schumann was amused. "Is that a fact?" he asked, sitting back in his chair. "It may interest you to know that Reich Marshall Goering himself selected the Brandenburg String Quartet to be *Valkyrie*'s musical entertainment for this season."

"Oh, well then... I suppose that explains everything." An indifferent shrug. "Everyone knows Party officials cannot err."

An instant later he winced and jerked slightly. I believe Elsa had kicked him in the ankle. The damage was already done, though. Schumann had caught the implied insult, and another jab at the Nazis couldn't be ignored. "And you believe you could do better, Dr. Einstein?" he asked, no longer affording him the dignity of addressing him as *herr doktor*.

"Of course. No question whatsoever."

"Then perhaps we should give you the opportunity of joining the quartet as a guest accompanist." Schumann gave him a tight smile. "I'm sure your fellow passengers would be thrilled to witness a performance by someone as illustrious as yourself."

"Albert..." Elsa began.

"It's all right, my darling." Albert gently patted her hand as he returned the captain's smile. He knew a challenge had been made, and he didn't hesitate to accept. "I would be only too pleased to do so, Captain Schumann," he said, then looked over his shoulder at Oswald. "Lieutenant, would you be so kind as to return to my suite and retrieve my violin? You'll find the case in the bedroom closet."

And this was how, a little more than an hour later, I found myself sitting beside Albert and Elsa in the front row, watching as the Brandenburg String Quartet made their way through *A Little Night Music*. The solarium was filled with passengers who'd come for the performance, and with the lights dimmed and cool blue moonlight streaming in through the plate-glass windows high above, the deck had become something surreal, a conservatoire ten thousand feet above the Atlantic.

Albert sat with his legs crossed and a finger raised to his lips, regarding the quartet as if studying an unknown species that had crawled into view from beneath a rock. The violinist who had given him offense was acutely aware of the scrutiny; the longer Albert stared at him, the more nervous he became, until his bow trembled each time he laid it upon the strings.

Elsa must have noticed this, because at one point she leaned over to her husband and whispered something in his ear. Albert rolled his eyes, but he reluctantly nodded and, lowering his hand from his face, forced a smile. I was about to say something to Albert myself—like *cut it out, you're scaring the poor man*—when I caught furtive movement from the corner of my eye. Looking around, I spotted Graham standing at the edge of the audience, making small but urgent gestures to get my attention.

There was no person I wanted to see more than Nigel Graham. Quietly excusing myself from Albert and Elsa, I rose from my seat and quickly strode across the deck to where he stood. Graham started to say something to me, but I grasped his elbow and pulled him away. Albert was watching us curiously as I moved Graham behind a row of ceiling support columns. Shielded from the stage and the audience, I pushed him against the duralumin beam and planted my hand beside his head so he couldn't get away.

"Hello, Inspector Graham," I whispered, "or whoever you really are."

His eyes widened. "Sonny, I don't know what you're—"

"Oh, no. Don't get cute with me." The telegram I'd received from O'Donnell was in my pocket. I pulled it out, unfolded it, and handed it to Graham. "You're a long way from Mayfair, aren't you?" I asked as he held it close to his face to make out the words. "Or maybe you want to tell me there's two cops in London with the same name?"

Even in the half-light of the solarium, I could tell that Graham's face had become pale. He didn't say anything as he handed the cable back to me. I waited for an explanation, and after a moment he let out his breath and shook his head.

"Look," he began, "I know how this seems, and believe me, there's an explanation. But right now, you have to trust me. Einstein's life is in danger this very minute, and you're the only person who can save him."

"How can I trust you if—?"

"Listen to me!" He started to grab my jacket lapels, but I did it first. An instant later, he found himself slammed against the beam with my other fist ready to punch him into tomorrow. But he wasn't giving up. "Listen!" he hissed. Don't worry about me! Worry about Lieserl! She's here, right now... *and she's going to kill Einstein!*"

I'm not always the smartest pencil in the box, but I've got a knack for knowing when people are trying to pull my leg. And so far as I could tell, Graham—or whoever he was—was on the level. "How can you know this?" I demanded, keeping my voice low but not relaxing my grip on him. "Are you working with her?"

"*No!* I swear to you, I'm not! I... I just know that she..."

Applause from the audience. The quartet had finished the piece. Still keeping Graham pinned against the column, I turned my head a little to see what was going on. The passengers were still clapping when Captain Schumann walked forward, raising his hands for silence.

"*Danke schön... danke...* thank you," he said. "And now, as a special treat, we have a surprise this evening, a celebrity who will be joining the Brandenburg String Quartet for a special performance." He made a grand gesture to the front row. "Ladies and gentlemen, please welcome... Dr. Albert Einstein!"

Another round of applause, louder now, as Albert rose from his chair and sauntered to the stage. In his hands were the violin and bow Oswald had brought from his stateroom. A quick bow to the audience, then he took a seat in the small wooden chair that had been placed for him on the stage. Albert turned to the quartet.

"*String Quintet No. 3 in C Major*, if you please," he said, then cast a sour glance at the first-chair violinist. "Try to keep up," he quietly added.

A titter from those in the first few rows who'd caught the remark. The violinist scowled, but obediently exchanged his instrument for another viola as Albert nestled his own violin under his chin. He touched the bow to the strings, and there was a moment in which the room seemed to hold its breath. Then the first sprightly notes danced from beneath his bow, and an instant later the quartet joined in.

If Albert had never devised the Special Theory of Relativity or written any of the papers that overturned physics in the first decades of the twentieth century, it's possible that he might have become a first-rate concert violinist. The Brandenburg String Quartet was quickly reduced to journeyman status; its members were competent, yes, perhaps even gifted in a modest way, but if anyone ever doubted that Albert Einstein was a genius, they witnessed its physical manifestation in a performance that was both flawless and heartfelt. The audience sat breathless as Albert, captured in the moonlight, effortlessly soared through the Mozart piece.

So was I. And that's how I nearly missed Lieserl.

Fate was on Albert's side, though. She'd entered the solarium from the dining room and, keeping to the shadows, silently walked alongside the audience. She was less than twenty feet from the stage when she moved past the columns behind which Graham and I were standing.

"There she is!" Graham reached up to tear my hand from his collar. "For God's sake, man, get her!"

I noticed that she was holding a folded silk shawl in front of her, as if to conceal something in her hands. She must have heard Graham, for her face snapped toward us. Her eyes went wide when she saw me standing just a few feet behind her. A flash of recognition—she must have realized that I was the man she'd seen on the wharf earlier that day—then she turned away and, as Albert's bow weaved toward the closure of the allegro, bolted for the stage.

I didn't have time to bend down and retrieve the Colt from beneath my pants leg. Charging from behind the column, I threw myself upon her. Lieserl didn't hear me coming; she screamed and staggered forward as I wrapped my arms around her, and there was a soft thump beneath our feet as the long-bladed carving knife she'd been hiding beneath the shawl fell to the floor.

Men and women shouted as they turned to see a young woman struggling against a large fellow who'd grabbed her from behind. Some gallant fool sitting nearby jumped up from his seat. He was going to try and hit me, I think, but Graham got in his way. Then I tripped over the hem of Lieserl's skirt and we fell together to the floor, where she continued to twist in my arms, howling like an enraged animal.

Albert had stopped playing the second he heard her scream. Rising from his chair, he watched in confusion as the two of us fought just a few feet away. A couple of stewards were rushing to help me, and I caught a glimpse of Hans Lentz running down the center aisle, when Lieserl managed to push herself up on her elbows. Fighting me like a madwoman, her hair and dress in disarray, she looked straight at Albert.

"Johnnie!" she yelled, her mouth twisting into a maniacal grin. "Johnnie! My mother sends her best regards, Johnnie!"

Then the crewman and the Gestapo agent were all around us. I didn't see the look on Albert's face, but I did hear the harsh, discordant sound of his violin falling from his hands and breaking its neck upon the stage floor.

ix

I joined the *Valkyrie* officers who hastily ushered Albert and Elsa from the solarium and back upstairs to their stateroom. If I'd had a choice, I would have instead taken control of Lieserl, but Lentz beat me to it. He and a petty officer handcuffed the young woman and spirited her out of the room and down a companionway. I tried to follow, but Lentz wouldn't let me. Besides, Albert was my primary responsibility; I had to look after him and Elsa first.

Meanwhile, Graham had simply vanished. In the confusion following the attack, he disappeared into the frightened crowd of passengers. I had a lot of questions for him, too, but I had to remind myself that he wasn't my immediate concern. I could always find him later.

So I followed Schumann, Oswald, and the other officers who'd formed a triangle around Albert and Elsa seconds after Lieserl was pushed face-down against the floor. The officers hustled them to the nearest lift; I stayed out of the way until we reached Deck Eight, then reasserted myself as the Einstein's "traveling companion." No one objected; my true role had become obvious by then, and they were aware that, if it hadn't been for me, Albert would probably be sprawled across the solarium floor with a knife in his chest.

For his part, Albert was amazingly calm. He turned away the ship's doctor, insisting that neither he nor his wife had been harmed, and accepted Schumann's repeated apologies with a quiet smile and assurances that he wasn't to blame. All he wanted was some schnapps for him and his wife; that sent Oswald scurrying downstairs to the bar, and once the captain finally left a moment later, Albert quietly closed the door behind him, walked over to the sofa, and collapsed upon it like a man who'd just carried a twenty-pound bag of sand up a hill.

He stared into space for a long moment. His tux was rumpled, his tie was askew, and until then I wouldn't have thought it possible for his hair to get any wilder. He let out his breath, then gazed down at his empty hands.

"My violin," he murmured. "My poor, poor violin." He raised his eyes to look at me. "You don't suppose you could recover it, do you? I'd like to see if I could get it repaired, once we reach America."

"Sure, Albert. Anything..."

"Anything?" Until now, Elsa had been remarkably cool, saying little to anyone but simply allowing herself to be taken from place to place. In the privacy of her quarters, though, that was coming to an end. "Anything?" she repeated, staring at me in outrage. "Then find out who that woman was, and why she wished to murder my husband!"

My thoughts exactly. Before I could say more, though, she turned on Albert. "Why did she call you Johnnie? And what did she mean about her mother... Albert, was this someone else with whom you've had an affair? Is that what this is about?"

"I have no idea what she was talking about," he replied. "She must have been deranged."

I'd heard that mechanical tone many times before, seen that same blank expression, in countless interrogation rooms and jail cells. It was the voice of denial. Albert was a genius, but that didn't give him any special talent for lying.

"You have no idea who she was?" I asked.

"I've never seen that woman before in my life." Albert looked me straight in the eye, and I knew that this, at least, was true. Lieserl was a stranger to him.

"Have you ever...?" I began, but stopped myself before I could finish. I wanted to ask him if he'd ever heard of Lieserl Maric, but remembered what Graham had said to me: *Whatever you do, you must not tell Dr. Einstein or his wife that Lieserl is aboard, or even that you know her name!* Until I located Graham and talked to him again, it seemed prudent that I do as he said.

"Never mind." I turned to the door. "Look, I'm going to check on some things. The worst of this is probably over, but... well, stay in your room, and don't open the door for anyone except me, Lieutenant Oswald, or Captain Schumann. Okay?"

"Very well." Albert gazed out the window at the moonlight rippling across the dark waters of the Atlantic. I think he was more upset about breaking his violin than nearly losing his life. Or maybe there was something else on his mind. I twisted the doorknob to lock it, then left their cabin and headed downstairs.

Graham wasn't in his cabin. His roommate told me that he'd returned just long enough to change out of his dinner jacket and put on a sport coat, then left again. I went back upstairs and roamed the upper decks until I found him in a small barroom on Deck Seven just off the promenade.

He was sitting alone at the bar, staring into the drink before him. He barely looked up when I sat down beside him; I think he'd been expecting me to find him. "I imagine you have some questions," he said, and the thickness of his tongue told me that the whiskey on the bar wasn't the first one he'd had.

"Loads." The bartender started to come over, but I waved him off. "Let's start with the obvious... who are you?"

"I can't tell you that."

"You mean you won't," I said, and he shrugged: same thing. "All right, then. I'll call my friend Lentz and turn the matter over to him. I imagine the Gestapo will be interested to know there's someone aboard posing as a Scotland Yard inspector. Most likely he'll have you detained until the plane returns to Germany, then..."

"I'll tell you anything but that." Graham picked up a swizzle stick and idly swirled it around his glass. "Whatever else you want to talk about, we can... but not who I really am or where I come from. That's something I cannot tell you. Do we have an agreement?"

I'd been bluffing, and he'd called it. I didn't like dealing with someone who kept secrets, but if Graham was adamant about not allowing me to know his identity, there was little I could do about it. And I owed him for tipping me off about Lieserl. If he hadn't warned me, Albert might be dead.

"All right," I said, "let's try a different question. Who's Lieserl Maric, and what does she have against Albert?"

"Lieserl is his daughter."

"I didn't know he had one."

"No one does. He has two stepdaughters with Elsa, Margot and Ilse, and two grown sons from his first marriage, Eduard and Hans Mark. But before them, he had a daughter, too. Lieserl was born in 1902 before he and his first wife, Mileva, were married... but since Albert's parents didn't approve of the engagement and an illegitimate child would have ruined his chances of getting a position with the Swiss patent office, they kept the pregnancy secret. So Lieserl was born in Novi Sad, where Mileva's parents lived in Serbia, and a friend of hers adopted the little girl a short time later."

"That must have broken his heart."

Graham shrugged. "Who's to know? He never even laid eyes on her." He picked up his drink. "Albert did his best to eliminate all records of Lieserl's birth. Even Elsa doesn't know she existed, because he didn't tell his own family about her. When she was adopted, she took the last name of Mileva's friend, and therefore grew up believing that she was another woman's daughter." He smiled as he took a sip. "All these years, Little Lieserl has been in Albert's shadow... until now."

"How did she find out? That Albert's her father, I mean."

"After Albert and Mileva divorced in 1918, Mileva moved back to Serbia. By then, Lieserl was a young woman, still living with her adoptive mother and unaware that a famous man was her father. Mileva waited until she was full grown before she re-established contact with her daughter, and it wasn't until just a few years ago that she let Lieserl know the truth. By then, she had reason to hate Albert and turn her daughter against him."

Putting down the empty glass, Graham hunched forward to fold his arms together on the bar. "Albert has another secret," he said quietly, once I'd moved closer to hear him. "He wasn't solely responsible for the Special Theory of Relativity. Mileva had a lot to do with it. Although the concepts are entirely his creation, she did much of the supporting work. She was a talented mathematician, which is how they met when they were physics students in Zurich. Math bored him and she was better at it anyway, so she did most of the number-crunching..."

"The what?"

"Never mind." He shook his head. "Anyway, he should have shared credit with her. Around the time that his work was becoming known within the scientific community, their relationship was going sour, and not long after that their marriage came apart. Albert was always something of a ladies man, and when he started spending time with his cousin Elsa, Mileva left him and moved away. As part of the divorce settlement, Albert agreed to give her the money he'd receive if he won the Nobel Prize. The money eventually went to her, but he refused to acknowledge her contributions. So while he went on to become famous..."

"She was forgotten," I finished. "And eventually she told all this to Lieserl."

"That's pretty much it, yes." Graham slowly let out his breath; I could smell the whiskey. "Lieserl took her mother's maiden name in tribute to her, but that wasn't enough. When she learned that Albert was heading to America aboard this plane, that gave her a date and place when and where he would be, and an opportunity for her to..."

"Kill me."

I looked around, and found Albert standing behind us.

How long he'd been there, I didn't know. Sometime in the past few minutes, he'd quietly entered the bar and slipped up behind Graham and me, where he'd eavesdropped on our conversation. And it was pointless to ask how he'd figured out where we were. After all, he was a genius.

Hearing his voice, Graham slowly turned his head to peer at him. "Oh, God," he muttered, then closed his eyes and let his head fall on the bar. "Tell me this isn't happening."

"Very well, then... it's not happening." Albert had changed out of his formal wear into an old pair of trousers, a baggy sweater, his overcoat, and hat. In the dimness of the bar, he was an anonymous presence; only a few other people were in there, and no one recognized him. "And while you're hallucinating," he went on, "perhaps you could explain how you know so much about Mileva and my daughter."

"And how you knew Lieserl would be aboard and what she was planning," I added. "Don't tell me you got this information from Scotland Yard... we both know that's not true."

Albert shot me an astonished look. I shook my head, and he nodded in silent understanding: Nigel Graham wasn't who he'd claimed to be. Graham kept his head on the bar for another few seconds or so before reluctantly sitting up again. "I... can't. It's too dangerous for you to know these things. Too much would be upset."

Albert regarded him for a long, quiet moment. There was something going on behind those sharp blue eyes: a mind accustomed to delving into the nature of space-time was probing another mystery. "All right, then," he said at last, "let's go find Lieserl. Perhaps she'll have some answers."

Graham's mouth fell open. "No! You can't..."

"Of course, I can," Albert said. "Just try to stop me."

x

The bartender told us where Lieserl was probably being held: in the brig, next to the purser's office on Deck Four of the starboard pontoon. The petty officer who'd taken her into custody was standing guard outside. His eyes bulged when he saw Albert Einstein coming down the corridor, and although Graham's detective shield was bogus, it was real enough to get him to unlock the steel-reinforced door.

The room was small, plain, and windowless, furnished with only a small cot and a toilet. Lieserl lay upon the thin mattress; someone had away taken away her jewelry and shoes, and thin smears running down her cheeks showed where tears had ruined her makeup. She didn't react when Graham and I came in, and I'm not sure she even recognized me as the man who'd tackled her during the concert. But she sat up when Albert entered behind us, and for a moment I thought she was going to hurl herself at him again.

"Johnnie," she breathed.

"Hello, Lieserl." Albert caught the sidelong glance I'd given him. "Johnnie was her mother's pet name for me... don't ask why." A faint smile, and he added, "If I needed any more proof that you're my daughter, that was it. How is Mileva, by the way?"

"She hates you more than ever." Lieserl's eyes bore into him. She remained seated on the narrow bed, but every muscle of her small, slender body was coiled tight. Keeping my hands out of my pockets, I moved beside Albert, ready to grab her if she tried another attack.

Albert lowered his gaze and shook his head. "I'm very sorry to hear this. I never meant her any harm. Your mother was my little Dollie, and for a time... including when you were born... she and I were very much in love. But I suppose she's never..."

"If you loved her so much," Lieserl snarled, "then why did you abandon us?" Her fists bunched, she moved a little closer to the edge of the bed. I cleared my throat. That was enough to warn her not to try anything. A wary glance in my direction, and she sat back again. "Why did you abandon *me?* Tonight was the first time you've ever seen me, father! It took trying to put a knife in your heart for you to acknowledge my existence!"

"I know... and giving you up was the worst mistake I ever made." Albert couldn't meet her gaze. He'd taken off his hat when we came in; now his hands nervously rumpled its brim, twisting it out of shape. "It was a stupid thing that we did... that I did... putting you up for adoption. I should have immediately married your mother and told my family to go to hell if they didn't like it, and accepted the consequences if the Swiss patent office rescinded their job offer. But—" an embarrassed shrug "—we were young and immature, and didn't want the responsibility of..."

"Don't blame her! Mother wanted to keep me!"

"No." Albert sighed as he raised his eyes to look her straight in the eye. "I'm sorry, but that's not true. She's probably told you something different, but think for a moment... if she'd really wanted to keep you, then she would have remained in Zurich and had you out of wedlock. Instead, she went back to Novi Sad to live with her family until she delivered you, because she knew that this way she'd find someone in her home town who'd take you without anyone in Switzerland being the wiser." He paused. "This was what we'd agreed upon, Lieserl. I didn't make her do anything that she didn't want to do... my Dollie had a stronger will than that."

"I don't believe you." But her voice was soft and shaky as she said this.

"I'm sorry, but it's the truth."

"But you... you denied her credit!" Just as it seemed as if it was being quelled, Lieserl's temper blazed forth again. "She could have become just as famous as you, if you hadn't denied her the right to be known as the co-author of your theories!"

"For the work I did through 1905... perhaps, yes. She did help me quite a bit, and I should have acknowledged her role." Again, Albert shook his head. "But when Elsa came into my life, Mileva very quickly went from being my wife and lover to my nemesis, and giving her credit for anything was the farthest thing from my mind. I'm sorry, my dear child, but she shares the blame for this as well. I only hope that she spent the prize money well."

Lieserl's mouth trembled. She looked as if she wanted to retort, but couldn't manage the words. In that instant, I saw a little of Albert in the intensity of her eyes. It was obvious that multiple thoughts, some contradictory of one another, were swirling through her mind; she was the child of two highly intelligent people, and had been poisoned by one of them.

At last she spoke, and it was only a whisper. "I hate you."

Albert didn't look away. "I never hated you. Perhaps I never loved you, either, but... there has never been a day that I haven't thought of you." A pause. "If things had only been a little different, we might..."

"What is going on here?"

In years to come, the world would learn that the Gestapo was neither subtle nor had a knack for good timing. I figured that out when Hans

Lentz unapologetically marched into the brig. Graham stepped aside as the Gestapo officer glared at Albert and me, arms folded across his chest. "I didn't authorize any visits with the prisoner. Remove yourselves at once."

Albert glared at him, irritated by the interruption. "The prisoner, as you call her, is—"

"Don't you think Dr. Einstein has the right to confront his assailant?" Graham cut off Albert before he could finish. "We don't even know who she is, or why she'd want to kill him... do you?"

Albert's gaze darted from Graham to me, and back to Graham again. Without asking, he realized that it wouldn't be wise to give Lentz any information he didn't already know. But was Lentz aware that this volatile young woman was Albert's daughter? Graham was clearly probing him to find out.

"No." Lentz's demeanor softened a little. "No, we do not. All we know is that the knife was stolen from the kitchen. I attempted to question her after we took her into custody, but she won't tell us anything except her name... Lieserl." He looked at Albert. "Have you ever encountered her before, Dr. Einstein?"

"No. I've never met her before in my life," Albert said truthfully. He turned to Lieserl again. "Have we ever met before? I cannot recall."

Lieserl was quiet for a moment. "No," she whispered, her voice so soft it was hard to hear. "I have never met Dr. Einstein until this evening."

"Then why did you attempt to kill him?" Lentz demanded.

Again, Lieserl didn't respond at once. She stared at the floor, her hands clutched between her legs. I held my breath, hoping that she'd realize, as I had, what might happen to her if she told an unconvincing story. The Nazis were willing to let Albert walk free of this aircraft once it reached New York, but if they became aware that Lieserl was his daughter, they might decide to detain her indefinitely for reasons of their own... perhaps as a hostage, thus making sure that he'd never do any scientific research for the Americans that might work against them.

I hoped she was smart, and a good liar, too.

"I... I don't know," she said at last. "I... there are voices in my head, I mean, telling me I..." She shook her head, then looked up at Albert and me. "Did I do something wrong? Why am I here?"

Albert's eyes widened, and for an instant I caught a glimpse of a smile beneath his mustache. "No... no, you've done nothing wrong. Not in the slightest."

Catching Lentz's eye, I cocked my head to a corner of the room. He nodded and stepped aside. "She's out of her mind," I murmured once our backs were turned. "Crazy as a bedbug, if you know what I mean."

"Plainly so, yes." Lentz nodded. "Once we return to Germany, she will be taken to a sanitarium where she can be admitted for treatment."

I'd overplayed my hand. "Well, I'm not sure if…"

"Pardon me… if I may?" Albert walked over to join us. "While I respect the efficiency of German hospitals," he said quietly, "I happen to know an outstanding doctor in New York, a psychiatrist who specializes in the disorders of the mind. If you'll release the young lady to my custody… or at least the custody of the New York authorities… I'd be willing to take her to my friend and recommend that she undergo treatment. At my expense, of course."

Lentz was hesitant. He gazed thoughtfully at Lieserl, evidently weighing his options. "It would make a lot of sense," I added. "This way, we'd have a better chance of keeping this matter under wraps… just a minor incident that happened en route. If she were sent back to Germany, though, the newspapers…"

"No. You are correct." Lentz quickly shook his head. It was clear that he didn't want to do anything that might raise the interest of the press and cast his government in a bad light. Getting rid of Lieserl in America was in his best interest. "Thank you for the offer, Dr. Einstein. Your generosity is appreciated."

"As is your sympathy and understanding," Albert said drily.

The irony was lost on Lentz. Nodding slightly, he turned toward the door. "Herr inspector, as a representative of Scotland Yard, is this a satisfactory… herr inspector?"

Looking about, I saw no one behind us except the petty officer standing watch in the corridor. Sometime in the past several minutes, Graham had vanished.

xi

I didn't see him again for the rest of the flight.

The remainder of the trip was uneventful. I took Albert back to his stateroom and firmly told him to remain there with Elsa until we reached

New York. He didn't object and neither did his wife. His close brush had sobered both of them. So they didn't roam the ship, but instead spent the following day reading and looking out the window at the ocean, with their meals delivered to their room by stewards.

I spent most of my time playing bodyguard, although by then it was obvious that they were out of danger. Lieserl was the only person aboard we'd needed worry about, and she was under lock and key in the brig. Albert didn't tell Elsa what he'd learned about the identity of his assailant; so far as she was concerned, the young lady who'd interrupted her husband's performance was a mentally disturbed stranger, nothing more or less.

Albert had made sure of that. "Elsa doesn't have to know about Lieserl, does she?" he asked as I walked him back upstairs to his room.

"Not unless you tell her. Will you?"

He was quiet for a moment. "Perhaps... but not yet. I need to figure out what to do about her... my daughter, I mean." He gave me a sharp look. "You'll help me get her off the aircraft once we reach America, yes?"

"Of course," I said, and a telegram to O'Donnell took care of that detail. When the *Valkyrie* landed in the Hudson the following evening, two plainclothes New York police officers were waiting on the dock to take Lieserl into custody. Lieserl Maric was the first person to leave the plane; no one on the dock paid attention to her as she walked down the gangplank on Lentz's arm, her handcuffs hidden by her overcoat sleeves. I watched from a porthole as she was helped into the back of a police car parked dockside; she never looked back, and I never saw her again.

Not in person, anyway. But I'd see plenty of her in times to come. We all would.

The press was waiting for Albert. They surrounded him and Elsa as soon as they came ashore; their arrival in America was heralded by camera flashes and the shouted questions of reporters, each of them wanting to know the same things: *Are you leaving Germany for good, Dr. Einstein? Are you fleeing Strasser?* Albert smiled and waved and gave non-committal answers; no one knew about the attack the night before, and when they found out, they chalked it up to a random assault by a crazy person, barely worth a column inch.

I quietly walked alongside Albert and Elsa, holding up a hand to ward off the more intrusive newspaper hounds, until we reached the sedan awaiting him on the wharf. Before he climbed into the back, he turned to me.

"Thank you, Sonny," he said, holding out his hand.

"You're welcome, Dr. Einstein," I replied. "Good luck to you."

"And you," he said. And then he was gone. The Packard drove off into the cool Manhattan night, carrying him into history.

I returned to the dock and watched the passengers as they disembarked from the *Valkyrie*. While the plane was still in the air, I'd left Albert's suite a couple of times to go down to Graham's room. He never returned to his quarters, though, or so his roommate told me, and a tour of the public areas failed to turn him up. The RF-01 was a mammoth aircraft, though, so there were plenty of places for him to hide.

Even so, I didn't see him get off the plane. Somehow or another, he managed to disembark without being spotted... by me, at least. I even went over to where the passenger baggage was being unloaded from the cargo hold. I found a suitcase with his name on the tag, but it went unclaimed. I stuck around a little while longer, then decided that this was one of life's little mysteries that would remain unsolved. My job was done. I picked up my bags, hailed one of the last cabs at the taxi stand, and told the driver to take me to my place in Queens.

That should have been the end of the story, but it wasn't.

xii

A few weeks later, I was cooling my heels at my office on West 53rd Street when there was a knock at the anteroom door.

I was there alone that day. My partner was on a job and our secretary had called in sick, so it was left to me to stick around to answer the phone. An unexpected visitor was a welcome break from the magazine I'd picked up at the newsstand down the block; I could see his silhouette through the door's frosted glass panel.

"Come in," I called, and dropped the new issue of *Black Mask* on my desk. The door opened, and who should walk in but the ghost who went by the name of Nigel Graham.

"Hello, Sonny," he said. "Long time, no see."

I stared at him for a couple of seconds. It actually took me that long to remember him. It had been just over a month since I'd flown back from England with Albert, and since then I'd handled several jobs. It was sometimes hard to remember the details of every single case my partner and I handled, even those left hanging. Then I recognized Graham, and had to control the impulse to jump up from my seat and grab him before he got away again.

"Hello, Nigel," I said, "or whoever you are. Who are you, anyway?"

"Nigel Graham is as good a name as any. The police officer I borrowed it from doesn't seem to mind." He took off his hat and motioned to the leather chair in front of my desk, the one our clients used when they came to see us. "Mind if I sit? It's just a social call this time, but I think I owe you a visit."

"What you owe me are explanations." But I nodded toward the chair anyway.

"I know... and I apologize for that." He removed his overcoat and folded it across the arm of his chair before sitting down. "It was necessary for me to make myself scarce just then... back on the *Valkyrie*, that is, when you and Dr. Einstein were questioning Lieserl and that Gestapo officer showed up. If any of you had asked me the wrong question... such as the ones you'd asked already... then it could have influenced the outcome in—" a moment of hesitation, followed by a shrug "—let's call it an even more unexpected direction. So I took the opportunity to disappear, and made sure than none of you found me again."

"I was wondering about that. How did you get off the plane anyway? And where were you hiding? I looked all over the place."

"Did you know there's a couple of lookouts... sort of like crow's nests... built into the wing stabilizers on each end of the plane? They're put there to help the crew make landings in tight places, but no one ever uses them." A rueful smile. "Rather cold, but I managed to remain hidden there until we reached New York. I found an extra pair of overalls in a locker, so I put them on and posed as a crewman when we landed. All I had to do was jump aboard one of the tenders that came out into the river to meet the plane and ride it back to shore."

"Slick, very slick," I said. "Almost as fancy as the stunt you pulled in the first place." He gave me a questioning look. "Posing as a Scotland Yard cop," I added. "What was the point of that?"

"Ah! Well... that's sort of the whole point of everything, isn't it?" Resting his elbows on his knees and clasping his hands together, he bent a little closer. "Hiring you as Dr. Einstein's bodyguard, getting you on the *Valkyrie*, making sure that you knew about Lieserl and the danger she posed when I couldn't persuade you to keep him away from the concert that evening... almost as if it was all anticipated, wouldn't you say?"

"I don't know, pal... you tell me."

Graham didn't respond at once. Looking about, he spotted the mystery magazine on my desk. "See, it's like this," he said as he reached over to pick it up. "People tend to think of the universe as being one big place that just goes on and on forever, but it's really not like that at all. In reality, there are many, many universes—literally countless—coexisting at the same instant on parallel planes, like the pages of this magazine." He ruffled the pulp's unevenly-cut pages. "They're separate from one another, but at the same time they're related, with events in one often influencing the events in others in discrete yet noticeable ways. Understand?"

"Yeah. Sure."

Still smiling, he closed his eyes and shook his head. "No, you don't. Most people, when they learn about multiple universes—the multiverse—for the first time, tend to disbelieve it. It's not something that's obvious with the naked eye. Even Dr. Einstein doesn't quite believe it, and yet it's his special theory of relativity that spawned the underlying science of quantum mechanics. Albert called it—or rather, *will* call it, in just a year or so—'spooky action at a distance'."

"You're talking about all this as if it happened in the past."

"For me, it *did* happen in the past. Or rather, in the past of your page of the multiverse." He held up the magazine again and opened it to a page at random. "This is your universe—" he flipped to another page at random "—and this is the one I'm from. Understand?"

"Uh-huh. I think so." On one hand, I'd pegged Graham as a crackpot. On the other hand, he was a pretty damned persuasive crackpot. Either way, I figured that it couldn't hurt to hear what he had to say. It wouldn't be long before men in white jackets showed up to take him back to the farm. "Go on."

"As I said, often certain events—and certain individuals—influence the outcome of parallel events in other planes of the multiverse, No one really knows why this happens. It just does. In this instance, one of those keystone individuals is Albert Einstein, who—in this page of the universe—was supposed to have been stabbed to death by his estranged daughter while traveling to America in 1933. This incident altered the course of history in tragic ways that I can't tell you..."

"Oh, of course not."

"What I *can* tell you, though, is that your own actions changed events in an unpredictable fashion." Graham rifled through the magazine again. "When you didn't shoot Lieserl—which is why I gave you the gun, so you'd end her life before she murdered Albert—you created a new page that didn't previously exist."

"Whoa... okay, stop right there." I held up a hand. "Look, I've been putting up with this, buddy, but you've just jumped off the deep end. Are you saying you came back through time...?"

"Not 'back through'... across. From one time-frame to another."

"Through, across, whatever." He was starting to confuse me... which was strange, because that could only mean that I was actually beginning to believe this stuff. "What you're telling me is that you'd set things up so that I'd kill Lieserl..."

"And therefore prevent worse things from happening, yes." Graham nodded. "As I said, I can't—or rather, I refuse to—tell you exactly what that is. However, I'll let you know this much: in most pages of the multiverse, it's important that Albert Einstein remain alive through the middle of this century, because of the crucial role he'll play in the outcome of major events to come."

"Uh-huh." I was no longer hoping the men in the white coats would show up. They might take me, too.

"That's why I came over here and posed as a Scotland Yard detective: to lure a previously uninvolved individual such as you into taking the steps necessary to save Dr. Einstein. But saving both him and Lieserl wasn't what we anticipated."

"And who is 'we'?"

"A group—a secret organization, if you will—dedicated to preserving human existence in all planes of the multiverse." As he spoke, Graham dropped the magazine back on my desk, then reached into a vest pocket. "We operate in subtle ways, and sometimes it's necessary to recruit contemporary inhabitants—or residents, as we call you—to work for us so that our hand will remain unseen."

Pulling out a metal card folder, he flipped it open and withdrew a white business card. "You've got talent, Sonny," Graham said as he stood up. "Talent we may need to call upon again." He placed the card face down on top of the magazine. "Keep this somewhere safe. It may be useful to you sometime in the future."

I didn't pick up the card, but instead watched as he pulled on his coat. "Just one more thing," I asked, and he nodded. "You said that saving both Albert and Lieserl changed everything. What do you mean by that?"

Graham picked up his hat, gazed at it thoughtfully. "I can't tell you that either," he said after a few moments, "but I'll give you something to think about. Lieserl is a little crazy, but she's most definitely her father's daughter. Now, imagine the possibilities of Albert Einstein reaching some sort of reconciliation with her, and then having a protégé to follow in his footsteps."

"I'm not sure I understand."

"Live long enough and you will." Graham put on his hat, walked toward the door. "Goodbye, Sonny. Perhaps we'll meet again."

The door closed behind him, and I reached across the desk to pick up the card. Embossed on it was: **QUANTUM MECHANICS, INC.**

Nothing else. No street address, no phone number. Just a white cardboard rectangle with three words. Or so it seemed.

Spooky events at a distance. That's what Graham said Albert called this sort of thing. I thought about calling him in New Jersey and asking him to explain it to me, but decided against it. Even he might not believe me.

So I dropped the card in my desk drawer, and waited to see what would happen next.

About the Author
ALLEN STEELE

Allen Mulherrin Steele, Jr. became a full-time science fiction writer in 1988, following publication of his first short story, "Live From the Mars Hotel" (*Asimov's,* mid-Dec. '88). Since then he has become a prolific author of novels, short stories, and essays, with his work translated into more than a dozen languages worldwide.

Steele was born in Nashville, Tennessee. He received his B.A. in Communications from New England College in Henniker, New Hampshire, and his M.A. in Journalism from the University of Missouri in Columbia. Before turning to SF, he worked as a staff writer for daily and weekly newspapers in Tennessee, Missouri, and Massachusetts, freelanced for business and general-interest magazines in the Northeast, and spent a short tenure as a Washington correspondent, covering politics on Capitol Hill.

His novels include *Orbital Decay, Clarke County, Space, Lunar Descent, Labyrinth of Night, The Jericho Iteration, The Tranquillity Alternative, A King of Infinite Space, Oceanspace, Time Loves a Hero* (former title: *Chronospace*), the Coyote Trilogy—*Coyote, Coyote Rising,* and *Coyote Frontier*—the Coyote Chronicles—*Coyote Horizon* and *Coyote Destiny*—*Spindrift, Galaxy Blues, Hex,* the young-adult novel *Apollo's Outcasts, V-S Day, Arkwright,* and *Avengers of the Moon.* He has also published six previous collections of short fiction: *Rude Astronauts, All-American Alien Boy, Sex and Violence in Zero-G, American Beauty, The Last Science Fiction Writer,* and *Tales of Time and Space.*

Orbital Decay received the 1990 Locus Award for Best First Novel, *Clarke County, Space* was nominated for the 1991 Philip K. Dick Award, and *V-S Day* was nominated for the 2015 Sidewise Award for Best Novel.

Steele's short fiction has appeared in most major American SF magazines, including *Asimov's Science Fiction, Analog,* and *Fantasy & Science Fiction,* as well as in dozens of anthologies.

His novella "The Death of Captain Future" received the 1996 Hugo Award for Best Novella, won a 1996 *Science Fiction Weekly* Reader Appreciation Award, and received the 1998 Seiun Award for Best Foreign Short Story from Japan's National Science Fiction Convention. It was also nominated for a 1997 Nebula Award by the Science Fiction and Fantasy Writers of America.

His novella "'…Where Angels Fear to Tread'" (upon which *Time Loves a Hero* is based) received the Hugo Award, the Locus Award, the *Asimov's* Readers' Award, and the *Science Fiction Chronicle* Readers' Award in 1998, and was also nominated for the Nebula, Theodore Sturgeon Memorial, and Seiun awards.

His novelette "The Emperor of Mars" won the 2011 Hugo Award for Best Novelette and also the *Asimov's* Readers' Award.

His novelette "The Good Rat" was nominated for a Hugo in 1996, and his novelette "Zwarte Piet's Tale" won an AnLab Award from *Analog* and was nominated for a Hugo in 1999. His novelette "Agape Among the Robots" was nominated for the Hugo in 2001. His novella "Stealing Alabama" was nominated for a Hugo in 2002, and won the *Asimov's* Readers' Award for that year. His novelette "The Days Between" was nominated for a Hugo Award in 2002 and a Nebula Award in 2003. His novella "Liberation Day" and novelette "The Garcia Narrows Bridge" both won the *Asimov's* Readers' Awards in 2005. His novella "The Legion of Tomorrow" won the *Asimov's* Readers' Award in 2014.

In 2013, Steele received the Robert A. Heinlein Award in recognition of his writings promoting the exploration of space. He was First Runner-Up for the 1990 John W. Campbell Award, received the Donald A. Wollheim Award in 1993, and the Phoenix Award in 2002. He has also received the 2007 Alumni Achievement Award from New England College.

Allen Steele is a former member of the Board of Advisors for the Space Frontier Foundation and the Science Fiction and Fantasy Writers of America, and he is also a former member of the SFWA Board of Directors. In April, 2001, he testified before the Subcommittee on Space and Aeronautics of the U.S. House of Representatives, in hearings regarding space exploration in the 21st Century. "Live from the Mars Hotel" is among the many stories and novels included on the "Visions of Mars" disk aboard NASA's Phoenix lander, which landed on Mars in 2008.

He lives in western Massachusetts with his wife Linda and their dogs.